HOLDING ON TO LOVE

HOLDING ON TO LOVE

ASHISH SINHA

Srishti
PUBLISHERS & DISTRIBUTORS

Srishti Publishers & Distributors
Registered Office: N-16, C.R. Park
New Delhi – 110 019
Corporate Office: 212A, Peacock Lane
Shahpur Jat, New Delhi – 110 049
editorial@srishtipublishers.com

First published by
Srishti Publishers & Distributors in 2020

10 9 8 7 6 5 4 3 2 1

Acknowledgment

I will forever be grateful for the motivation and positivity I could draw from the thoughts and beliefs of Brahma Kumaris. These beliefs aided me to get over the hardest time in my life.

To my wife, who stands with me for everything I do – I thank you and I am honoured to have you in my life. Your overwhelming love, contentment, acceptance and sacrifices helped me sail swiftly through the days of endurance. Your financial independence allowed me to take some time off my work and focus on my recovery, giving me time and space to dawdle over my writing skills.

To Maa – without you, I'd have no foundation to build lovable families.

To the memory of my beloved Baba and Papa – thank you for instilling in me the moral values to help me become the person I am today.

To Stuti – thank you for taking interest in my story and marking up my work, helping me with the useful edits. I really appreciate her suggestions and creativity in framing this wonderful book.

To Dr Joy and his competent team at Global Hospital – for making an intractable surgery a success. Thank you for the care, kindness and concern you showed during my long stay.

Lastly, to everyone who is reading this book – your support, motivation, reviews and critiques will be appreciated.

Ashish Sinha

Prologue

In my mind's eye, I could see the people of Delhi as though I was flying above them. It was Holi, and there were people everywhere, crowding the streets; some running, some walking and lots of children splashing colour on each other. As far as the eye could see, the crowd went on, dotted with food carts selling delicacies like malpua and dahiwada – my personal favourites.

I could hear the thela owners calling out to attract people, and children shrieking. Strangely, even though I was flying above them, their voices seemed too close. And when I stopped flying, I felt the weight of my body… and then the bed beneath me as well, pressing upward as if to swallow me. I groaned, thinking, 'It was all a dream.'

But as I took a breath and steadied my mind, I heard the children shriek again, and I could smell the wonderful aroma of food wafting from my kitchen. The flying may have been a dream, but Holi was real, and it was today. Now!

I shoved aside the bedclothes, preparing to go to the window and look at the happiness outside. But I felt the all too familiar aches and pains, the slight dizziness, and an overall fuzzy feeling in my head. For months I had been steadily inching toward liver failure, and the symptoms of my chronic liver disease were fluctuating wildly with every passing day.

I somehow managed to get to the bedroom's balcony. Pushing aside the heavy curtain, I winced at the bright sunlight and steadied myself with one hand on the door frame. Blinking, I looked down to see a boy – not unlike myself when I was younger, though taller and thinner – running to catch a group of his friends. As he approached them, he launched a bucket of colour into the air. The water fell, mostly splashing one of the girls, but also sending droplets of crimson across their friends' clothes. Even with my physical discomfort, I could not stop a smile from spreading across my face as the girl turned and ran directly at the boy.

'Ashu!' Disha called out to me from the kitchen. 'Come, try this food!'

'Coming!' I called back, but only half-heartedly. Due to my dietary restrictions, I knew it would be something almost oil-less and salt-less. How could anyone enjoy Holi like that!

As this question crossed my mind, it was followed by others which had tormented my mind since my diagnosis. 'How long before my liver fails?'

'How will we afford a transplant?'

'Where will a new organ come from?'

And the ever present, 'Why?'

My anxiety level had been steadily increasing as my symptoms seemed to grow more severe with each passing week. My wife Disha always did her best to cheer me up – she is an amazing woman of strong faith. Yet my mind, well… it seemed have a mind of its own.

I stumbled into the kitchen, stretching and moaning as I fell into a chair. 'It smells delicious,' I said.

Disha turned, holding a bite of food on a fork in her hand. 'It is delicious, I am telling you.' She smiled that beautiful smile I have come to treasure, and popped the bite into my mouth. The scrumptious flavour spread across my tongue even before I got a chance to chew.

'What is it?' I mumbled with my mouth full. 'It's… tasty.'

'It's dahi bada,' Disha responded. 'I found the recipe on the internet; they say it is not too bad for people with liver troubles.'

As I swallowed the bite, my stomach grumbled, and I realized that I was truly hungry for the first time in days. 'Is there more?' I asked, not waiting for her answer as I scanned the kitchen counter.

Disha laughed. 'You're such a foodie…'

'So are you!' I retorted as I squinted at the oven door. 'I see some in the oven.'

'Yes,' Disha said. 'I'm keeping it warm until the others get here. We will eat some, then go and play with colours.'

'No playing with colour,' I groaned, half out of disappointment at having to wait for the food, and half in my uncomfortable state. 'You know I should stay away from crowds.' As I said it, I thought to myself, 'That's as good an excuse as any – I'm just not up for it.'

No sooner were the words out of my mouth that I felt cold water hit my right side. Stunned, I froze, then slowly turned my head to face its source. Standing at the kitchen door was Shrawan, Disha's brother.

'That does it,' I growled, getting to my feet and grabbing a glass to fill at the sink.

'Come out,' Shrawan shouted as he ducked back toward the hallway. He began whistling happily, his tune fading as he made his way back to the stairs which would take him down to the crowd.

'We really should,' Disha said. 'It will do your spirits good; you love Holi.' She turned and lifted a couple of buckets, full of coloured water. Her eyes twinkled as she held one out to me.

'More dahi bada first,' I said, accepting the bucket and tilting my head playfully. Disha lowered her eyes but she was too late – colour washed over her before the words had left my lips.

'Oooooooh!' she shrieked. She took a step back and hit me full force with some of the colour from her bucket. I ducked slightly and hit her from another angle, laughing.

'You said no playing with colour!' Disha pretended to be offended, but then brought from behind her back a glass with some new colour. Before I could even tell what colour it was, she had showered me with it.

'What's all this ruckus?' It was my mother standing at the kitchen door this time. We looked up at her sheepishly as she slowly scanned the room. After taking in the mess, she started shaking her head. 'You are such children!' she shrieked, then pulled a towel from the counter and began soaking up the colour.

'Maa,' I said, 'It's Holi. You can't expect us to suddenly grow up on Holi.' I grinned, dipping my fingers into colour and spritzing her with it. She snapped the towel at me as I grabbed Disha and pulled her out of the kitchen.

'Let's go,' I said. 'Suddenly I think I'd like to go down to play...'

'Anything to avoid cleaning,' Disha giggled. We turned and made our way down to the crowd.

❖

Disha is an amazing woman. She is playful like a child on occasions like Holi, and mature and sophisticated at the workplace. I have watched her cook and care for my family members, design and decorate our apartment, and encourage our nieces and nephews. In the four years of our marriage, I have come to admire and love her beyond words.

When we first learned that my liver was failing, we were both devastated. It seemed that our short life together had come under threat, and that our remaining time as a couple would be spent in endless tests and hospital visits. It certainly was not something we expected at such a young age.

But in a day or two, Disha was able to shake off the shock and began to put together a strategy for success. One of her first goals was to pull me out of the depression which had taken over me, and she made a concerted effort to convince me that my negative thoughts would only make things worse. She seemed to know exactly what was needed to raise my spirits, and thanks to her and her family, even my worst months became memories I now treasure.

This is my story… our story.

This book has been dedicated to my treasure, my Disha. She is my darling, my wife – and the strength of my life.

Chapter I

Early Life and Family

हरा / Hara (Green) : peace, stability; immaturity

'Please remain still,' the nurse said before sharply jabbing a needle into my arm. I watched my blood flow into a tube, and then into another as she switched the vials.

My mind was racing, but my hand was steady. 'Good,' I thought, 'no one can see how nervous I am.'

I had every reason to be nervous. Today was the day I would receive a new liver. A donor had been located; the organ was compatible; we were ready to proceed.

I looked up at the wall and saw a poster hanging there. 'BE SAFE – DISPOSE OF ALL SHARPS' it proclaimed to the room. Looking back over at the nurse, my eyes met hers as she withdrew the needle, disengaged the last vial, and dropped the 'sharp' into the bin.

'Be safe,' I thought. Those two words seemed to sum up my life, in more ways than one. Since leaving ICU, my topmost priority had been keeping away from any possible source of illness. But the words meant more than that to me. 'Be safe.'

I had taken my fair share of risks since my childhood. The baby of my family, I had been loved and doted on by my family and relatives. Although we had suffered loss and hardship, my parents had provided for me well. More than anything, they had arranged my marriage to a wonderful woman, whose faith in god (Shiva) was the only thing that had prevented me from sinking into deep depression in the face of this liver disease.

Today, I would be going into surgery to replace that failed organ. My very life was on the line.

'Could this be my last hour?' I couldn't help the thought entering my mind. I began to wonder how different my life would have been if fate had been merciful. If I hadn't known the kind of courage and strength Disha and her family taught me as we faced my illness together.

'Bygones are bygones,' I thought as I rolled down my sleeve, nodded my thanks to the nurse, and turned towards the door.

❖

1.1 Spotty memories of the past

'He's gone.'

I heard my uncle, but my mind had gone numb. My heart sank. Terrible memories of similar words echoed from my past. 'How many times,' I thought. 'How many times must a man hear that a beloved person in his life has died?'

This time it was my father – the man who had set the course of my life. Papa was dead, and I knew our family would never be the same.

We – my uncle, some relatives, and I – had been in the car on our way to the hospital in nearby Patna, having been told

Papa's health had taken a turn for the worse, and his liver was failing. After hearing my uncle's words, I have no memory of how I got from that car to our house. Before I knew it, an ambulance was pulling up in front. Inside it was Papa's body, along with my brother, my sisters, and Maa. My brother got out of the ambulance first, and I fell into his arms, overwhelmed with grief. Sobbing, we made our way back to Maa, where I did my best to comfort her.

She was overwhelmed with grief, and also with worry. Papa and Maa did not have an ideal marriage. Theirs had been an arranged marriage, like mine. But unlike mine, the struggles between the two of them had been plenty. Maa's impoverished upbringing had left her full of worry in financial matters; worry which did not subside, no matter how diligently my father worked to support our family. For years, she had warned him about saving for the future, but Papa had his own ideas about how money should be managed. Now he was gone, and she mourned his loss, knowing it was too late for financial plans.

My understanding of family – prior to Disha's coming into my life – was quite different. I was raised by Fua (my aunt) and her departed husband's father, who I call Baba. My parents and siblings lived in another home nearby. Our town was not large – it was one of those 'sleepy' towns where things rarely change. Life there could be harsh, at times, but as a child, it was all I knew, and I have many fond memories from that place. Looking back, I now count myself lucky to have had early experience with the harshness of life.

❖

1.2 The Patriarch

'Take some food out to the driver,' Papa said, handing me a plate piled with food from our dinner. 'Tell him to share it with our colleagues in the back seat.'

I dutifully carried the plate out to the car, which was parked and waiting in front of the home I shared with Fua and Baba. I was used to this routine, as my father would always nosh to his friends or family.

Since before I was born, Papa had been the 'patriarch' of our family. He had four brothers, two of whom were employed in government jobs, but financially it was Papa who provided the 'bread and butter' for everyone.

'From Papa,' I said, handing the plate to the driver. 'He says you all can share it.'

The driver took the plate and handed it over his shoulder to one of Papa's colleagues. I recognized him, but not the other man sitting next to him.

'Thanks,' the stranger said. He pulled a piece of bread from the plate and began to eat hurriedly.

'Tell your Fua we always enjoy her cooking,' said the driver. I nodded and turned back toward the house.

Papa was always up for providing for everyone – family, and others as well. Not everyone understood, but I know this was done out of generosity and love for his family. He knew that if he did not, each of his brothers would take their families and go their separate ways. Without his financial support, the house would disintegrate, we would grow apart. For him, keeping the family united was of more value than money. He was the glue that held us together.

Fua was Papa's sister. She and her deceased husband's father had made a home for me. In many ways I was the child Fua never had. Papa made sure that I wasn't left wanting anything, by supplementing the meager pensions Baba and Fua got.

I went back into the house. Fua was washing dishes while Baba and Papa sat at the table, reviewing a newspaper.

'Fua,' I called, 'they send thanks, and they say they always enjoy the food.' I saw her shrug her shoulders in response. She rarely showed it, but I knew she was grateful for the compliment.

'They should,' Baba said. 'It's the best payment they could get for their services.'

Papa chuckled. 'Those guys would eat anything,' he commented. 'But they're good as gold. Not everyone would put up with me.' He took his last bite and pushed his plate away.

I knew my father loved me just as much as I loved him, but he wasn't the kind to show affection. He also came across as harsh to us at times, but I think this was because nothing had come easily for him. Having started out as an assistant in a chemist shop, he had gone on to become an officer in the sales tax department. The fruit of his hard work was shared by all, but I'm not sure our family fully appreciated the effort he made to keep us together.

I took my seat beside Baba, who handed me a part of the newspaper. A few moments passed in silence as I ate. Once done, I gathered the soiled plates and carried them over to Fua at the sink, still reading as I walked.

'Dinner was delicious, Fua,' I said. 'You are the best cook in the house!'

She scowled at me. 'I'm the only cook in this house,' she hooted. 'You would all starve, if not for me!' She tapped my head with the spoon she had been drying. I grinned at her and sheepishly hid behind the newspaper.

My father was also a very good cook. I carry very fond memories of him cooking scrumptious food and inviting all his friends and relatives.

If Papa was the glue in our family, Baba had always been the heart. After losing his own son (Fua's husband) years before in a fatal road accident, Baba looked upon me as the grandson he never had. He and Fua doted on me, and they had essentially adopted me. As far back as I can remember, I always lived with them, and they gave me a loving home.

❖

1.3 Baba: the heart of my childhood

'Faster! Faster!' I shouted, tapping Baba's head with a twig I had found.

'It's fast enough,' Baba panted, but he sped up a bit anyway. Baba suffered massive elephantitis in his legs: they did not carry him; it was the other way around! And for the moment, he was carrying me, too. I bounced on his shoulders as he lumbered from the house to the veranda and back again. I was only four, but this was a game I already knew well.

'It's my turn,' one of my cousins called from the veranda. 'Ashu has been riding forever.'

Baba turned away from him and started towards the house again. 'Be patient,' he said over his shoulder. 'You'll get a turn soon enough.'

Whenever I got into disputes with my cousins, Baba always came to my defence. When I made mistakes, Baba always put things right. He was generous to me, giving me lots of love and gifts. Baba was not a rich man; his only income was a small pension. In spite of this, anything I ever asked for, he made sure to give me the very next day.

'Baba,' I leaned down to whisper in his ear, 'will you please buy me a game console?'

Baba groaned and sat heavily on the steps leading to the house. I climbed down from his shoulders and sat beside him.

'What's a game console?' he asked.

Playing video games on your television set had become a popular pastime for kids my age. My friends and cousins played these games in their homes, and I really wanted to have a game console, too.

'It plugs into the TV and you play video games on it!' I replied. 'Everyone else has one. Can I have one too?'

Baba gave me a stern look. 'Everyone else has one is not reason enough to get something,' he commented, shaking his head. He looked over his shoulder toward the door to the kitchen, then over to my cousin, and back to me. He shrugged, then leaned down close to my ear. 'I'll see what I can do,' he said softly.

Looking back, I have to laugh at how precocious it was to ask for such a thing. It was rare for kids in our small town to receive something as expensive as a game console.

A week passed, but I heard nothing more on it. I had just begun to wonder if Baba had forgotten about the game console, when he came home with a box in his hands.

'Open it!' he said, handing it to me. I saw his name on the label.

'Is it from Patna?' I asked, pulling at the tape on one side.

'It is. I picked it up there today,' said Baba. 'I wonder what it could be. Hurry and open it!' He put a very serious look on his face.

I scrambled to tear the remaining packing tape from the box, discarded some papers from inside, then pulled out one joystick and then another.

'A game console!' I shrieked. 'I thought you have forgotten about it!' I pulled the console out, then game after game from the box, eagerly reading each label.

'I will never forget you, Ashu,' Baba said into my ear, hugging me close to him, then planting a kiss on the top of my head.

I truly felt I was the most favoured kid in the entire neighbourhood, because I was loved by Baba, Fua, Papa and Maa, by all my relatives, friends, and even Papa's colleagues. (To this day, I wonder if Papa had something to do with getting that game console.) I had cousins to play with, and a brother and two sisters who cared for me. Life was good.

❖

1.4 Loss of an upholder

'He's gone! He's gone!' We could hear Fua moaning from the other room.

My cousin and I dropped our joysticks and looked at each other with wide eyes. We leaped to our feet at the same time, and for a brief moment I revelled in the fact that I was a head taller than he was. At school, we were both starting to compete in games. 'He may be faster,' I thought, 'but I have greater endurance.' But putting aside these thoughts, worried over Fua, we raced to the kitchen. We saw her staggering toward the table, still wailing, telephone in hand.

'He's gone! Baba's gone!' She broke down into tears, dropping the telephone receiver to the floor, and covering her face with her hands.

I froze in my tracks, not believing my ears. Baba? Gone? It just couldn't be.

My cousin hefted Fua's right arm and glared at me. 'Get her other arm,' he muttered. 'We need to get her to a chair.'

In a daze, I picked up Fua's other arm, stumbling as she fell toward me and leaned on me with her full weight. I was a head taller than her too, but in my shock, it took me a moment to react.

'Wait!' I exclaimed, staggering before catching myself to support her. 'What… what happened?' She raised her head, somewhat found her feet, and looked over at me past her hunched shoulder.

'It's Baba,' she wailed loudly. 'He's gone… he's dead.' Her moans became deep sobs, and she sagged once again. It took all our strength to hold her up from falling to the floor.

Together the three of us shuffled over to the table, and my cousin eased her down into a chair. Seated, she folded her arms on the surface of the table and continued to sob.

I was none too steady myself. Bracing my arms on the table's surface, I slowly lowered myself into a chair next to Fua. 'It's just not possible,' I thought. 'Baba has always been there. He just can't be gone.'

I sat numbed in silence, getting callous to the questions my cousin was bombarding on my uncle, trying to get the details of the mishap. Fua's moans echo in my mind every time I am reminded of her loss. She was left all alone on losing Baba, and all the condolences offered to her were of little comfort to her.

❖

1.5 Social obligations

Life is not always cakewalk. It has its ups and downs; and we have successes and failures, loves and losses. I was barely a teenager when I lost my Baba. In many ways, his passing pulled the rug from under my feet. I felt I'd lost my pillar of love and strength, my guardian, my torch-bearer. How would I find my way forward in life without him? Fua would do her best to support me, of course, but losing Baba truly left me feeling orphaned.

I stayed in shock for weeks, if not months. Being the only male left in my household, the social obligations and rituals after Baba's death fell onto me.

I made arrangements in a daze. I had Baba's body moved to our house verandah as a part of custom followed by our family. I also informed other family members and notified the officials about the death. As food arrived, Maa and Fua busied themselves arranging dishes on the serving table. Fua had recovered somewhat and seemed to be better when busy with work.

'Keep an eye on her,' Maa whispered to me, pulling me aside. 'I see some people over there I need to speak to.'

I nodded and went over to Fua, putting my arm around her. 'The food looks good,' I said. She peered up at me with sad eyes.

'It does,' she said. I could see in her eyes that the grief still had her fully in its grip; she was saying the words, but they had no meaning for her.

'Why don't we fill a couple of plates and sit?' I asked. She nodded and we proceeded to do just that. At the end of the table, I grabbed two bottles of water and motioned toward some chairs nearby. She obediently sat in one of them as I settled into another.

'Life will not be the same without Baba,' I said, sighing sadly. Fua started to cry again, softly this time, and I put a hand on her arm. 'Thank you for helping with the food,' I whispered in her ear. 'We can use all the help we can get.' She seemed not to hear me, but nodded and wiped her nose with a napkin, sniffing. Once recovered, she silently picked up a piece of food and took a bite. Maa approached us and stood next to my chair.

'Ashu, please come with me,' she said. 'Your Papa and I need to discuss something with you. Your cousin will sit with Fua.' Maa took my plate from me, making it clear that this was something which could not wait. I stood to follow her, and my cousin took my seat. Maa and I made our way back to the table, where Papa was filling his plate.

'Ashu,' Papa said without looking up. 'I know it is hard losing your Baba.'

'Yes, Papa,' I answered, trying to stay composed. I stared down at Papa's shoes as he continued.

'You are the head of your household now,' he said, looking up at me suddenly. Determined to remain calm, my eyes held his, but a deep sense of fear began to creep up inside me. What was he saying? Hadn't I done what I needed to do? Hadn't I taken care of the rituals? Was I missing out on something?

'Yes, Papa,' I responded, keeping my voice as steady as I could. Just then, Maa put her hand on my arm, so I looked over at her. She moved her head, motioning toward the chair where Fua sat, still nibbling on the same piece of food.

'You must look out for her,' Maa whispered. 'She needs you now.'

'Fua is your responsibility now,' Papa said, clearing his throat. 'We will do what we can to help you, but it is important that you understand this.'

Their meaning soon became clear to me. The loss of Fua's husband at a tender age, and now her father, had taken its toll on her, leaving her emotional and dependent. Papa and Maa were trying to tell me that I could never view Fua as my guardian; she would be depending on me for everything, and not the other way round.

Papa and Maa continued to be supportive as we grieved Baba. They stepped in and helped me, and Papa began to weave dreams for me, for my future. Before long, I felt able to make decisions more independently, and the household with Fua became less of a burden. Papa made sure all our material needs were met, but no one could ever fill the void created by Baba's demise.

Now Papa was gone too. Life would never be the same again. I did my best to comfort Maa, to be the pillar of support she'd be missing, just like I had with Fua. But she was inconsolable in her worry over the future. My brother and I understood. More than anything else, we feared that the glue that had held our family together, was gone.

❖

One important function of the liver is to process nutrients the body needs.

हरा / *Hara (Green) : peace, stability; immaturity*

Childhood is such a carefree time for those surrounded by loving families. We are fed, clothed, and sheltered, with little awareness of how those provisions are obtained. We often take our parents and family members for granted, thinking they will always be there, and sometimes faulting them when we do not feel loved. But their provision for us is meaningful – it is their very lives that they pour into giving us the things needed in life. The fact that they perform their duties consistently is, in itself, a statement of how much they love us.

I was loved abundantly as a child. I was surrounded by family and friends who cared. But the tragedies of life can wear down even the most loving relationships; and, for some, the loss of loved ones can make it more difficult to find love in their hearts for others.

I did not fully understand Fua's grief over Baba; I was too lost in my own. It was not until I lost my own father that I understood her devastation – the desperation of losing one's rudder in life.

As I grow older and face troubles of my own, I sometimes ask myself, where are all of those friends and family members who loved me as a child? Where are all of those friends and colleagues who were helped by Papa? But I know where they are: mourning those they have lost, working for their families, and doing their best to surround the next generation of children with an environment of love.

Many of us, whether from the east or the west, are the product of traditions, of duty, or of responsibility, rather than beloved children of parents who share a loving bond. This can hold us back, if we let it. Life gives us a challenge: Can we view the act of providing basic essentials for our children as a form of deep love?

Those of us blessed to survive childhood are no longer confined by our origins. We can choose differently, and there is always hope for a better way to live. My Disha believes this, and lives it. Along with her family, she has shown me that we can approach life this way, together. This is a tremendous gift, for which I am eternally grateful.

Chapter 2

School and Friends

सफेद / *Safed (White) : mourning and rebirth*

Blood tests done, I opened the door to the waiting room, but I was a bundle of nerves. 'What will happen?' I asked myself. 'Will I really get a new liver today?'

I approached Disha, trying to hide my anxiety. She was scrolling through her phone, looking perfectly composed. 'She always seems so confident,' I thought, almost envying her. 'But beautiful too.' I wished I could tell her how grateful I was for everything she had brought to my life – for her strength and her faith that had never wavered. Since the day of my diagnosis, she had told me god would take care of me, and now, it seemed maybe it was true. 'I must try to show the same confidence today,' I told myself. 'I will tell her how nervous I was when we are through with this.'

Her eyes met mine and I could see that she was nervous too. Not in a way that changed her confidence; just in a caring way, knowing that the next 24-48 hours would be unlike any other in our lives. 'The doctors should arrive soon,' I said. 'Then we will know what to do.' She nodded.

I sat next to her and held her hand. I could feel her pulse. It was comforting, but fast, like my own. Together we sat quietly, waiting.

❖

2.1 Nonchalant days of childhood

'Ashu! Ashu!'

I heard Fua's voice from across the field close to our house. She had been calling me home for dinner, but it was such a beautiful day, and our kite was sailing through the sky so effortlessly, that I had lost track of time.

'Ashu, I am not going to warm up the food for you. Not again,' she almost screamed. 'Come home now!'

'You better go in,' one of my cousins whispered. 'She doesn't sound too happy.'

'You're right,' I responded. I knew that Fua's asthma made it difficult for her to cook over the hot stove, and I did not want to upset her more. 'I'm coming!' I called out aloud. She had already turned to go back into the kitchen by then.

I reeled in the kite as quickly as I could, taking care not to let the wind break the string. Once the kite was safely back down, I waved goodbye to my cousins and ran back to the house.

As I walked into the kitchen. I could sense from her face colour and expression that she was more upset than I had expected.

'Give me that!' she snapped, taking the kite's spool from my hands. She snapped it into two and threw the pieces into the corner of the room. 'There are more important things than kites,' she said, 'and eating is one of them. Now finish off everything on your plate.'

Sheepishly, I put my kite aside and took my seat next to Baba. He had continued eating, pretending not to have seen or heard anything. I knew that Baba was sympathetic towards me. He knew I preferred playing over everything, and he was just making sure I live my childhood to the fullest.

❖

2.2 Following my passion

A few years later, a group of us were playing cricket in the field near the house. This was another of our favourite pastimes. I played cricket extensively, and had reached the district level games by the time I was in 7th standard.

One particular day, I was the striker, waiting to hit the ball. My cousin was the bowler, gearing up to throw the ball towards me. I had to save my wicket, to make sure the team did well. But the fielding team had been on its toes; they had dismissed a lot of players very swiftly. I was strategizing in my head, wondering how I would tackle the incoming ball. I was determined to hit the ball out of the field and score maximum runs for my team.

My cousin lobbed the ball towards me and I swung the bat with all my might. I started running to score more runs, but in my mind I was convinced that it was a great shot. I watched the ball sail over the heads of the fielding team. I ran as fast as I could, celebrating in my mind the runs our team would be earning.

I had reached the middle of the pitch when I heard both teams shout – 'No, no!' A glass shattered somewhere. Although I completed my run to the other end, I knew something had gone very wrong. I followed everyone's gaze in the direction of the ball; I winced at a broken window not far from the door. Before I could do anything, my brother came out of the house, carrying the ball.

'Ashu,' he said out loud. I didn't like the tone of his voice, so I hesitated. He spoke again, 'Come here!' I hung my head and ran towards him, still carrying my bat. My brother reached down and pulled it from my hands.

'You broke the window. The game is over for you,' he said.

With that, he suddenly hit the bat on the road with full force, snapping the bat into pieces. I felt a combination of confusion, anger and disappointment; my heart was still beating hard and fast from the exhilaration of the play.

'I'll fix the window,' I said, panting a bit from the run. 'You didn't have to break the bat.'

'Nobody will say anything to you; they will make me fix the window,' he said. 'This way,' he said throwing the broken bat on the road, 'you'll remember what you did.'

He turned and walked back to the house. Picking up the pieces of the bat, I looked out of the corner of my eye at the two teams on the field. They stood, waiting and watching. But my brother was right; with one bat gone, the game was over. For now.

❖

2.3 Compulsion of studies over shinning talents

Soon afterward, Baba sat me down for the conversation he had been putting off for long. I was to enter the eighth standard soon, and it was time for me to begin taking my studies more seriously.

'Ashu,' Baba started gently. I can still hear his resonant voice, and the love he always poured into saying my name. 'Ashu, you are a good boy,' he said. 'I know how much you like to play.'

'Yes Baba,' I said. 'Cricket is the best game ever. Someday I will be a great cricket player! I will make you all so proud.' I swung an invisible bat in the air, then shielded my eyes and looked afar, watching an invisible ball sail over imaginary trees in the distance.

Baba chuckled. 'I am sure,' he said, smiling and motioning for me to sit next to him. 'You will be a great cricket player. But Ashu...' he paused, reaching over and taking my wrist. He pulled me closer to him and said lovingly, 'You know Ashu, I liked to play cricket too.'

Silently, I moved my eyes to his gigantic legs, swollen with elephantitis. I tried to imagine him as a boy like me, long before his legs grew so large, striking the ball and running. The thought made me sad, but I listened carefully, knowing from the tone of his voice that he was trying to tell me something important.

'All kids like to play, but now you are growing up now.' Baba pointed toward the kitchen, where we both knew Fua was preparing the meal. 'Your Fua and I do what we can to keep this house going,' he said. 'I fix things when they break, and you know your Fua works hard to make our food.'

I nodded, still wondering what he was trying to say. Did he want me to help with those things? In my mind, I thought, 'Whatever Baba wants from me, I'll do it.'

'Ashu,' Baba said again, and the love in his voice was overwhelming as he said my name. 'You are growing up, and as a young man you have to do your part, too.'

'Yes Baba,' I said, rising to my feet. In my heart and mind, I was already doing whatever I could.

He paused for a moment, then finally broke the silence. 'Your part is to do your studies… sincerely,' he said.

'What?' I asked, incredulous. This was not what I had been expecting, and for a moment I thought I had heard him wrong. 'My studies?' I checked.

'Yes,' Baba said. 'Games are fun, but they will not feed you and the family. You have to learn now so you can work to bring in money, and our bread and butter, when you grow up. You can only do that by paying attention to your studies right now.'

Confused, I sat back on the steps next to him. 'But Baba, we already have money, and bread. I don't understand.'

Baba chuckled. 'Yes, Ashu,' he replied, 'we have bread and we have money because your father is a generous man. But someday he will not be able to work to give us these things. Someday your brother and you will have to do it.'

I leaned against Baba's arm, thinking about what he had just said. To me, these things – having money and food – had just happened. I had never considered exactly *how* they happened.

After listening to him, I stood up tall in front of Baba. 'Of course, Baba,' I said, and in my mind this matter was already settled, though I didn't fully understand why. Baba smiled and nodded, and took my hand again. 'You're a good boy,' he said. He arose with some difficulty, heaved one leg around the other, and lumbered slowly into the kitchen, leaving me to ponder over his words.

When I think back on that event now, I feel it is a mistake to stress the importance of studies over the talents demonstrated by a child. How many great cricket players are discouraged in their youth? How many great musicians or artists? Rich families often encourage these things in their children, but we need to find ways to search for hidden talent in middle class families as well, to bring it to light. The cricket great Mahendra Singh Dhoni of Ranchi comes to mind suddenly, but we need to find more ways to discover such talent.

That said, I did as promised and began to focus on my studies after the conversation with Baba. When he passed away, my father did his best to make sure that my needs were met, and to pave the way for me to progress academically and get into a reputed school. And I did well, successfully gaining entrance into Delhi Public School in Ranchi.

❖

2.4 Living away from family

'Wait up!' I called out to a group of my friends. They had left the classroom before I had packed my bag, and now I was running to catch them. They had a strange look about them – they were walking very close to each other, as if not letting even air pass between them, and taking small steps.

'What's going on?' I asked as I got nearer.

'Shhhh!' One of the boys looked over his shoulder at me.

'Ashu, be quiet!' said another.

I soon caught up with them and saw that they were huddling around one of the boys. They were all looking down at something he had in his hands.

'What is it?' I asked quietly, peering over to see what the excitement and suspense was all about.

'Shh!' A boy in front of me raised a finger to his lips, then motioned his head toward the other boy's hands. I saw him attempting to light a cigarette with a lighter. The wind kept putting out the flame, so the boys were pressing closer to him, trying to block the wind.

'Ohh!' I exclaimed, not quite knowing how to react. Baba and Fua had always told me that smoking was a bad thing, that I should not do it. They didn't tell me exactly why, but I always knew that if I smoked, I would be in trouble.

'Where did you get it?' someone asked.

'My father smokes,' the boy in the middle said. 'I snuck three of them from his pack. And my brother bought me the lighter. He smokes all the time.' He brought the lit cigarette up to his lips.

I looked at all of them one by one. We had only known each other a few short weeks, but in that time I had come to like them. I did not want to see them doing something I knew was so wrong. Some of them looked worried, but others seemed excited, and I still did not know how to react.

One of the boys finally spoke up, 'Well, my family doesn't smoke, and I don't think you should either,' he said. 'It's against the rules. You'll get us all in trouble.' He started walking faster, pulling the sleeve of the boy next to him. A couple of other boys walked ahead with him, while a few hung back.

I decided it would be best to ignore both groups. 'Let's race,' I said to the boy next to me, and tugged on his sleeve.

'Okay,' he responded, and together we ran toward our rooms, relieved to be away from the whole situation.

My initial time in Ranchi was much like any student's first years away from home, I suppose. I was not a very disciplined student;

my friends and I wasted many hours talking, watching movies and partying. But as the end of school approached, I knew I would have to get serious if I wanted to pass the final CBSE exam – a standardized test all 12th graders take. While at home prior to the exam, I locked myself away in my room to focus and study, and somehow I managed to get a 70%, which was a passing grade. Next came entrance exams for college, which are much more challenging.

❖

2.5 Coaxing Papa

'Ashu,' Papa said in his stern voice. 'You passed your boards, but now you must get ready for the entrance exams.'

'Yes, Papa,' I said. 'I know.'

'I think you should join some coaching classes and prepare properly,' Papa said. 'There is a coaching centre in Delhi that is very good. Or you can go to the one in Kota. They will help you – you need to study.'

I considered this carefully, knowing Papa only wanted the best for me. How I wished Baba was still alive; he could explain to Papa how much I needed the love of my family, how much I had missed them when I was away at secondary school in Ranchi. While school was in session, I had only been able to talk to them once a week, and even then only about my immediate needs. Now that I was back home, the last thing I wanted to do was leave Fua and my siblings and cousins again. I needed the encouragement of my parents and the love of my family.

'Papa,' I started, then hesitated, trying to choose my words carefully. 'Papa, please let me stay here. I will study hard on my own, I promise.'

'Yes,' Maa chimed in quickly, 'he can do it here.' I looked over at her, initially surprised at the unsolicited support, but then I realized she was mainly concerned over the expense. I looked back at Papa's face. His brow wrinkled as he considered the matter.

'Well,' he said, 'you managed to pass the boards. If you study as hard for the entrance exams, I suppose you will be okay.'

'Yes, Papa,' I said, knowing this was the best decision. 'And,' I added, 'I will get into a great private school for engineering.' Engineering was Papa's dream for me, so I knew my saying this would please him.

'Private schools cost more,' Maa interjected. 'The government ones are just fine.'

I tried not to let my expression change, and I kept my eyes fixed on Papa's. I wanted to go to a private college in general; I thought they had better facilities. But good government schools had a better reputation when it came to campus placements, and they were now at par in terms of facilities. Somehow I had my heart set on attending a private college, maybe because it was comparatively easier to get an admission into private school, given you had money. Government schools required high degree of competition for gaining admission and very few were able to crack the entrance test. Disha was among the few.

'Papa,' I said, 'I will study hard. I will do well in the entrance exams, and I will get into a good private college.' I looked directly into his eyes, hoping he could see how determined I was.

Papa held my gaze for a moment, then dropped his eyes to his hands. After another moment, he looked over at Maa. 'You heard Ashu,' he said. 'So we will see.'

I would have loved to end this thread by saying that I had as much success with the entrance exams as with my boards, but that was not to be. Not long after this conversation, Papa fell sick. Before we knew what had happened, he was gone from our lives. This event, above all others, completely changed the course of my life. In my mourning and grief, I missed the exams that year. And I got another chance at it only one whole year later. Everyone knew it was my last chance to fulfil Papa's dream of my getting into engineering.

Earlier I had chosen not to take coaching for entrance exams, now I had no option but to prepare on my own. Papa was a generous man, but he had not put aside much for the future, so our family struggled without his income.

❖

The liver makes millions of molecules of proteins every day, synthesizing them as needed to keep the body healthy and functioning.

सफेद / *Safed (White) : mourning and rebirth*

Death is a difficult thing for anyone to cope with, at any time. But for a youngster, it can be devastating, especially if they lose a parent. Children need their parents; they need love and encouragement; they need their parents to be involved in their lives.

Papa's death left me without direction, and although my immediate family supported me, other family members did more to discourage and disappoint than to help. Their thoughts were not for me and the difficulties I was facing without Papa's help; they were more concerned with money and their own desires.

In my grief and disappointment, I fell into bad habits and got involved with friends who in many ways hindered my path. Without Papa's guidance and any strong support, it just seemed easier to turn to cigarettes and alcohol than to walk the path he had laid out for me.

Thankfully, these wayward years did not deter me permanently; they did set me up for a lot of further worry after I was diagnosed with liver failure. Before tests determined the cause, I couldn't help but wonder if beer drinking had contributed to my failing health. The same family members who had discouraged my taking the entrance exams speculated that alcohol had killed Papa and was making me ill too – but that wasn't true.

I really feel life is a series of waiting rooms. What counts is what we do in those rooms.

One of my resolutions going forward is to make better use of precious hours, days and months; contributing to relationships and to the world in ways that will last; ways that will make us all better people. Having a brush with death puts a lot of life into perspective: our time here is short, and we have to make the most of what we have been given.

My plan is to adopt Disha's approach of thinking positively and believing in the good things in life which make us all richer – not just in finances, but in uplifting experiences and meaningful friendships. I intend to carry on my father's legacy of generosity, sharing what I can and weaving a better future for those around me.

Chapter 3

Illness and Papa's Death

भूरा / *Bhura : Brown*

Disha must have seen the doctor enter the waiting room the same time I did, for we both jumped to our feet at once. 'Everything is set,' he said. 'The liver is here, we have a room waiting for you, and the blood tests look good.' I took a deep breath and exhaled a sigh of relief. This was not the first time we thought an organ was coming; sometimes even when one becomes available, it doesn't work out.

'Please follow me – we must prep you for surgery.' Disha and I followed him down the hall to the nurses' station. They exchanged a few comments, then the nurse turned to me. 'I'm sorry, your wife will need to wait out there,' he said, motioning toward the waiting room. 'You can take a moment to say goodbye. Your room is right through those doors. We will be ready for you.' He pointed to a pair of doors over which the sign read, 'OPERATING THEATRE' then bowed his head slightly and walked through them.

'I guess this is it,' I said to Disha.

'Yes,' she said softly. 'It will be all right. I will be waiting to see you after.' I grabbed both her hands, trying to stay composed. 'This may be the last time I see her,' I thought. I tried to memorize her face, her hair. My throat closed, and I cleared it.

'Yes,' I said, leaning over and kissing her lips quickly. She lowered her chin; a subtle move telling me to stay confident, but her eyes betrayed her own fears. Only a husband can see this in such a strong woman.

'Stay positive,' she said. 'Think of a successful surgery. Think of a full recovery.' I nodded my head and turned.

'I'm so lucky to have her,' I thought, and went through the doors.

As I entered the room where the nurses waited, I felt like a lamb going to slaughter. They began preparations, removing my clothing and wiping my body down with cold antiseptic cloths. In my mind, I was reviewing other trips to the hospital. My thoughts turned to my father's illness, my brother's accident, and their deaths.

'Thoughts are important,' I could hear Disha's voice saying. But the memories were clear; insisting that I let them have their way with my mind, even as the nurses were taking control of my body.

❖

3.1 Dawn of devastation

'I don't feel well,' my father said, stumbling into the kitchen. His skin was yellowed, even more than usual, and he was gasping in short breaths. We had all noticed how unhealthy he appeared: he had been gaining weight steadily, even though we rarely saw him eat.

My mother held her hand to his head. 'You're burning up!' she exclaimed. 'Boys, get in the car – we will take him to hospital!' My brother pulled the car around, and I helped Fua into the passenger seat as Maa guided Papa into the back. We all drove as quickly as we could to Patna, the nearest town to our home, where the hospital was located. Papa grunted as we hit bumps and made the turns to get to the hospital.

'Take it easy!' he groaned, holding his stomach, his face drawn up in a grimace. Maa raised the back of her hand to his forehead again.

'Does your head hurt?' she asked, as he winced with her touch.

'Everything hurts,' he said shakily, leaning against the door of the car. 'It feels like my body is going to explode.'

We pulled up to the hospital, and Maa and I rushed Papa into the emergency room. I stood in a queue to get Papa registered. After a brief wait, my brother arrived after parking the car. Soon, we were ushered into an examining room. Fua and Maa were mumbling to each other, and I guided them to chairs near one of the walls. Once they were seated, I turned to help my brother assist Papa, who was trying to climb onto the examination table.

'Step on that step,' my brother said to Papa. He held one of Papa's arms and most of his weight, while I was steadying him by the shoulder.

'Why is there a step?' Papa moaned. 'A person should be able to sit without stepping.' He lifted one foot onto the step, then hesitated a moment, took a deep breath, and held it while he shifted his weight to that foot and rose. My brother and I helped him turn so that he could sit on the table, which was actually more like a reclining chair. Once Papa was seated, my brother moved aside to lean against one of the walls. I stayed next to Papa, my hand still on his shoulder. He was not visibly shaking, but I could feel his body trembling. Fortunately, it was not long before a doctor came in to surmise Papa's condition.

'He's highly jaundiced,' the doctor said. 'The weight gain is likely due to the fluids he is retaining. We'll do some tests, but it looks to me as though his liver is failing.'

'What?' Maa said. She was having a difficult time processing what was going on. My brother waved toward the doctor to indicate that we understood, then turned to Maa. The doctor left the room, leaving a nurse behind with us.

'Maa,' my brother said, 'the doctor says he thinks Papa's liver is starting to fail.'

'I heard him,' she said mournfully, 'but what exactly does that mean?'

The nurse was drawing blood from one of Papa's arms while he remained reclined on the examination table. She looked up at Maa and said, 'We'll know more when these tests come back.' After filling several vials with blood, she deftly discarded the packaging and needles as required, then brushed past me out of the room. 'This shouldn't take long,' she said softly, and the door closed behind her.

'Papa,' I said, my voice quaking. The whole ordeal had me a bit shaken. 'Do you feel any better?'

Before he could answer, I heard Maa moan from her chair. 'Look at his belly!' She pointed to his stomach, protruding from him and nearly the size of a basketball. 'What's going on?!' She dropped her face into both her hands. Fua put an arm around her, but she was nearly just as upset.

My brother moved to Maa's other side and tried to comfort her, and I leaned over Papa, searching his face for any indication of what might help him. 'Can I do anything for you?' I asked. We all were feeling helpless. Papa had been trying his best to keep quiet, but his face still held the grimace – we could tell he was in pain.

'I don't know,' he said. 'I think we just have to wait for the test results.' He no more than finished speaking when the nurse returned carrying vials and more needles. She dropped them on a table next to Papa and began preparing two injections.

'I'm going to give you a couple of shots,' she said. 'The first is a diuretic; it will help your body dump some of that fluid from your belly.'

'I don't know what happened,' Papa said, and I could tell he was feeling as helpless as the rest of us. 'One minute I was fine, and the next, all of this…' He started to lift his hand, motioning toward the wall as if to indicate the room. The nurse inserted the first needle into his arm, and his voice trailed off.

'Just try to keep still,' she said. 'I'm also going to give you a slight sedative to help keep you calm.' Without hesitation, she put down the first needle and picked up the second. Before we had even processed what she was saying, the second injection was done and she had again discarded the needles and trash. 'We will have the blood test results soon,' she said, then turned and left the room.

At that point, time seemed to have stood still. Every now and then, Papa would moan and shift his weight on the examination table. The rest of us sat quietly, my brother and I checking our phones from time to time, performing web searches to try to learn more about liver failure. Every now and then, one of us would announce our findings to the other, but mostly we read silently.

Maa and Fua made small talk, nervously recalling what little they knew about other people who had suffered liver disease.

After what seemed like an eternity, Papa grunted and sat up. 'Find out where the restroom is,' he said, positioning himself over the step and obviously preparing to stand. The diuretics were apparently doing their job.

A couple of hours (and several trips to the restroom) later, we were all still seated in the room, doing our best to remain patient. We had been checking with the nurses every few minutes, but they only told us to stay in the room, each time saying they would come to us when they had the test results.

Finally, the doctor entered the room again, this time with a different nurse, who walked in with a wheelchair. 'Well, it looks like you're going to stay with us awhile,' he said. He flipped through some of Papa's records on a clipboard. 'Your liver does indeed appear to be failing; so we need to get you admitted. Then we will try to address all of your symptoms. Your ascites seems to be improving; you don't look quite as bloated as you did when you came in.'

'My what??' Papa asked sluggishly. He did look a bit better, and he had stopped groaning when he moved, but he was slumped slightly to one side. We couldn't tell whether he had improved or if all of this was just the effects of the sedative.

'Your ascites,' the doctor answered.

My brother looked up from his phone, where he had been doing a quick web search. 'He means your fluid,' he said. 'You got rid of some of the fluid in your body.'

'That's right,' the doctor said, nodding toward my brother. He turned to Maa. 'Ma'am, your husband is very sick. We're going to get him into a room, and then we'll be able to assess his situation better, but he will definitely need to stay overnight. You can go home and pick up whatever you think he will need. The nurse will show you to his room, and I'll check back in with him in half an hour or so, once he is settled. Do you have any questions for me?'

Maa hesitated, looking from the doctor's face to Papa's. She seemed disoriented and confused, so my brother spoke, 'We'll pick up some things for him, doctor,' he said, 'and when you check back, we may have a few questions then.'

'Very well,' the doctor said. He nodded to the nurse and turned towards the door. As he left the room, he called over his shoulder to Papa. 'Sir, don't exert yourself. Let them wheel you to the room, then stay in bed.'

'Thank you,' Papa mumbled, rising to his feet on the step. The nurse held his arm as he stepped down and then plopped down heavily into the wheelchair. My brother moved behind the chair while the nurse arranged his feet on two supports, and I moved between Maa and Fua, holding their hands as the nurse led us all to the elevator.

We followed the nurse out of the elevator, down a long hallway, and into one of the rooms. My brother pushed Papa's wheelchair to the bed. I looked around and noticed that it was a shared room, with a thick curtain blocking the view of a second bed closer to the windows. I could not tell whether or not it was occupied.

'There you go!' the nurse said as Papa settled into the bed. She leaned him forward and fluffed the pillow behind him, then eased him back against it. 'Comfortable?' she asked.

'Thank you,' Papa said, and I couldn't help but notice he had not answered the question.

'Can I get you anything else?' she asked, looking around at all of our faces.

'Maybe a bucket of ice chips,' Fua responded quickly. She had a bit of familiarity with hospitals, having stayed with Baba before he died.

'Of course,' the nurse said, walking back towards the door and left the room. My brother turned on the television, keeping the volume low, and began flipping through the channels as I guided Maa and Fua to chairs near the bed.

Now that I have familiarity with liver disease, I better understand the condition Papa was suffering at that time. Ascites occurs when blood fails to flow through the liver properly. Pressure builds up which makes the problem worse, and that is what was causing the pain Papa had been feeling.

Eventually the kidneys fail to remove excess salt from the body. This in turn causes fluid retention, with water accumulating in the abdomen, and ultimately swelling the feet and ankles. I understand the condition now, having suffered it myself later. More so, I don't understand why the doctors in Patna gave Papa just a diuretic instead of removing fluid from his abdomen with a needle that night.

'Well, we better go before it gets too late,' my brother said after a few minutes. He handed me the remote control and went over to help Maa back up out of her chair.

'Be sure to get a comb and toothpaste,' Fua said, then added, 'And shaving supplies.'

While my brother and Maa were gone to get what Papa and the rest of us would need for his overnight stay, Fua gave me a better idea of the bigger picture.

'You know how your Papa has been staying in Forbesganj?' she asked.

'Yes,' I answered. I knew he had rented a house there when he had been transferred in his job. 'I've visited him there a few times.'

'Well,' Fua continued, 'you probably don't completely understand why he spends so much time there... and why he comes to our house for dinner so often...' She hesitated, glancing over at Papa. He was snoring softly, having promptly fallen asleep.

'You mean when he comes with the car,' I said quietly. I could recall many nights when Papa had sent me out with food for his driver or for friends riding with him. 'He always says it's just because he doesn't want to wake Maa.'

'Psshaw...' Fua shook her head. 'That's just what he says. He's really avoiding your Maa. She wants him to stop using his money for everyone else.'

'Using his money?' I considered this thoughtfully. It was true that Papa supported a lot of people. He had always been the main bread-winner for our family.

'Right,' Fua continued. 'He pays for everyone and keeps very little for himself.'

'Keeps it back?' This was not something I had heard anyone talk about before. 'Keeps it back for what?'

'For things we don't expect, like visiting the hospital or other emergencies.' She shook her head, looking down at the floor. 'Your Maa has been worried that something like this would happen. Not necessarily to your Papa, but... you know... things like this happen sometimes.' She lowered her voice further. 'That's why he drinks... that's why his liver is bad!' she whispered.

'Maa never said anything like that to me,' I said a bit gruffly, starting to feel a bit uncomfortable discussing this with the two men in their beds next to us. Thankfully, I was saved from having to delve into the matter any further, because my brother and Maa came back into the room at that moment, shopping bags in hand.

I had known money was an ongoing issue on which Maa and Papa could not agree, but I had not realized that Papa was avoiding his house because of that. I also had not known that Papa had turned to alcohol rather than contend with their differences.

'He's starved for love,' I thought to myself, 'just as much as I have been, since Baba died.' Drinking may have helped Papa cope with the situation temporarily, but now the alcohol was taking its toll on his liver.

Once Maa and Fua had emptied the shopping bags and stored various items around the room, we discussed who would stay with Papa through the night. It was decided that we would take two hour shifts, with my brother and Maa staying in the room for the first two hours. Fua and I gathered up a few things and went back down to the waiting room. It had already been a long night, and it was going to get even longer.

This was January, and I had been preparing for my entrance exams. Even as ill as Papa was, he was still very concerned over my studies. When morning came, Maa came down and told me Papa was asking for me. As I entered his room, he was sitting in the bed, calmly reading a newspaper.

'You only have a couple of months before the exams,' he said. 'I don't want you wasting any more time here in Patna. Go home and study!'

I looked at him with concern. I did not want to leave him unless he was on the road to recovery.

'Go,' he said. 'I'll be fine. I'll follow you soon.'

I noticed he was clean shaven; I thought it was a good sign.

'All right, Papa,' I said quietly. What else could I say! 'Get better and come home soon.' With that, I turned and left the room.

At home, I did my best to concentrate. But I was exhausted from the long night at the hospital. Before the sun went down, I climbed into bed and quickly fell asleep. Just as I began to dream, all chaos broke out in and around the house.

'Ashu!' I heard Fua calling. 'Oh, Ashu!' I heard other voices too – loud voices, all talking so rapidly I could not make out what they were saying. I scrambled out of the bedroom and into the kitchen, which was filled with people. Everyone was on their phones; my uncle was talking to my brother.

'We're coming right away,' he said excitedly. 'We're on the way. The taxi is here.' He hung up the phone and looked up at me, his eyes filled with worry. 'It's your Papa,' he said. 'Your brother says his health is deteriorating again. We have to go to the hospital now.'

I was still blinking the sleep out of my eyes, trying to understand what was happening as my uncle pushed me toward the taxi. The telephonic conversations on the way were increasingly tense, and at last, my uncle broke down in tears. I could tell something terrible had happened, but he was so overwhelmed with grief that he could not speak.

For me, time stopped as it dawned on me that Papa must be gone. The taxi continued, but I had lost all my senses. I suppose I went into some kind of shock. The next thing I remember, we were back in my home town, and one of my neighbours was helping me out of the taxi.

In the house, the grief was overwhelming. My relatives were devastated; after all, they were as dependent on my father as I was. So in addition to grieving his death, they were panicking as they considered the prospect of moving forward without his financial support.

I was beside myself with sorrow. All my hopes and dreams seemed shattered. 'How can I go on in life without Papa?' I cried. I could not stop weeping and I was still crying when an ambulance pulled up outside and my brother and I fell into each other's arms. He tried to pull me to the ambulance, but I couldn't move. I could not imagine taking even a single step without the man who had instilled in me all of my aspirations and dreams.

Maa and my sisters were in the back of the ambulance, weeping loudly as my relatives helped my brother get me seated alongside them. My father's body lay covered in a sheet. I was so devastated with grief and sorrow that I could not even bring myself to lower the sheet to look at his face.

Together we hefted Papa's body onto our shoulders. 'He carried us on his shoulders when we were children,' I thought, tears streaming down my face. 'Now we carry him.' From a very young age, and all of my own life, Papa had carried the burden of responsibility for our family on his shoulders. As we carried him, my brother and I felt that burden full force. The weight of the household was now ours. Papa had shown us how to act as a guardian; now it was our turn.

We made our way from the ambulance to the veranda of our house, placing his body there so that people could pay homage, as is our tradition. For hours I sobbed as friends and family came to pay their respects. This went on the entire night, with my brother and me taking turns holding my father as we wept.

Our tradition when someone dies is to prepare the body through rituals called *sanskar karma,* leading up to cremation. Cremation in our culture is not just the burning of the body; many rituals continue for thirteen days. As my brother performed these rituals, it seemed as though everything remained dark for us. (This darkness continues, for our lives will never be the same.) But somehow the rituals settled me; I began to accept that Papa was gone and we would have to steel ourselves for life without him.

'Your Papa was a good man.' I looked up to see who was speaking. It was one of his friends, the owner of a sweet shop near our house. He continued, 'We will miss him.'

'Thank you,' I said. Just then, one of Papa's colleagues approached us. I remembered his face as one of the men who used to ride in the car when Papa would come to Fua's for dinner.

'Ashu, we are so sorry your Papa is gone,' he said, laying a hand on my shoulder. 'I want you to tell your Maa and Fua that they need not worry. We will take care of all of you.'

'Yes,' the sweet shop owner said. 'Your Papa was good to us; we will not forget it.'

I wiped the tears from my eyes, but more formed just as quickly. 'Thank you,' I said again, sniffling. 'I know Papa wants me to finish my education; that was the last thing he told me...' My voice broke and I started weeping again. It seemed the tears would never end.

'Of course,' said Papa's colleague. 'He always said you would go to an engineering college. He wanted that more than anything.' He removed his hand from my shoulder and patted my back. 'And you will finish college. No one is worried about that.'

As the thirteen days progressed, many friends and family members continued to come and go, many trying to console me by telling me I should contact them if I needed anything. Over and over, people assured me that they would support me in my studies.

One day, my brother asked me to contact the sweet shop owner. We were running low on food for the people. By this time, I had composed myself a bit. I cleared my throat as the phone rang.

'Sweet shop… how may I help you?' I recognized the gentleman's voice immediately.

'Hello,' I said. 'Ashu here.'

'Ashu!' he exclaimed. 'It's good to hear from you. I guess you are still having the *sanskar*?'

'Yes,' I said. 'That's why I'm calling. My brother says we are getting low on food today.'

'Low on food?' The man paused, and I wondered if he was waiting for me to say something else. 'Ashu, I think you should have your brother call me.'

'He asked me to call you,' I said. 'Is there a problem?' I said with some hesitation.

There was a long silence on the phone. 'Ashu,' then the man said, 'please just tell your brother to contact me. Now I have a customer, so I must go.'

'All right,' I said, reluctantly hanging up the phone. I went back into the yard, and quickly located my brother near the veranda.

'Will the food be here soon?' he asked. I shook my head.

'No,' I said. 'He says he needs to speak to you about it.'

'He wants money,' my brother said with disgust. He started walking toward the house, but stopped and looked at me over his shoulder. 'The *sanskar karma* is not even over, and he has already forgotten what all Papa has done for him!'

This was just the first of many disappointments. So many people had said they would support us, but all those turned out to be empty promises. Maa had been right, after all; the people Papa had so generously supported through the years – assisting them with marriages, construction of houses, food and other needs – all turned their backs on our family once Papa was no longer there to provide for them. Even the closest relatives.

In my grief and disappointment, I missed the entrance exams that year, but Maa and Fua scrimped and saved what they could from their meagre pensions to make sure I was able to take them the following year. I will always be grateful to them for helping me fulfill Papa's wish, if only a year late.

❖

3.2 Wrestling to gain admission

'Study, study, study,' my uncle said, shaking his head as he hovered behind me. I hunched my shoulders and stared intently at my book, determined not to let him distract me.

'Ashu,' he said, 'you should give this up.'

I turned a page and copied an equation into my notebook, trying my best not to let him get my attention. He was one of several members of my family who wanted me to forego the entrance exams and settle for a simple graduation course.

'I need to study,' I said in a low voice.

My uncle crossed the room to the sink, picked up a glass and filled it with water.

'The exams are so expensive,' he groaned. 'Your cousin took the graduation course and he is doing just fine. That is what you should do too.' He took a few gulps of the water, then turned back to the sink for a refill. 'Think of your Maa and Fua. They do not have the money.'

This was not the first time my relatives had discussed this with me. But Maa, Fua, my brother and I had agreed that it was important for me to fulfil Papa's wishes. They were willing to pool what they could from their incomes to cover the expense of the exams.

'I am thinking of them,' I said as I began working the equation on the page. 'Papa wanted me to go to a good college, and they do too. You already know this.'

'Sure, sure,' my uncle said. 'That's all well and good. But your Papa is dead and your brother is working hard. You should stay and help him.'

Pressure like this became almost constant from my relatives, making my preparations more difficult than they needed to be. Thankfully, Maa, Fua and my brother did manage to pull together enough money to pay for the exams. I was grateful that they understood how important it was for me to gain admission into engineering school. By god's grace (and with the help of a friend), I managed to meet the qualifying score for one of the reputed colleges in Orissa.

❖

3.3 Stress to perform

'Hey kid,' the senior yelled, walking towards us as we were heading to our class. 'What three-letter word starts with S and ends with X?'

'What a moron!' my friend whispered under his breath, then called out, 'SIX!'

It seems to be a rite of passage for new college students to suffer the torment of older ones, and things were no different in my college. I did my best to ignore them all, focusing on my studies and my father's dying wish that I succeed in engineering school.

The college turned out to be everything I was looking for – it had a large central library, a full-sized swimming pool, a large playing field and well-maintained living quarters. I set forth in my college career, my expectations for these 'golden years' dampened somewhat by my grief for Papa.

At my college, the freshmen were quartered far from the seniors in an effort to reduce the amount of 'ragging' or 'hazing' we had to suffer. The 'SIX' joke was just one example of the kind of taunts the seniors would make at us. I never faced any harsh treatment from them; sometimes they asked me these strange questions, but my friends and I were pretty good at coming up with answers that prevented us from receiving too much punishment.

I did well in my first year, studying hard and making a lot of friends. In the second year, we moved to a different building with a different dress code, and as we relaxed into a more comfortable environment. I became less focused on my studies and actually struggled for a long time. But ultimately, I didn't let Papa down – I pulled myself together and managed to graduate on time. I proudly accepted the engineering degree, knowing that Papa would be proud too.

'*Abey beer marega?* Want a beer?' My roommate, asked lighting a cigarette in our hostel room.

I was struggling to sleep, the thoughts of my family's struggle to support me taking over my mind. I knew how difficult it was for them. My sister had compromised a year before she took the MBA course so that I could have adequate funds for my fees.

The pressure to perform well in the examination kept me fretted; the frequent pestering and badgering by relatives didn't help. Somehow it instilled a feeling of guilt in my mind for choosing a profession that required lots of money.

So when offered a beer this time, I thought it was a soothing offer. I replied, 'Do you have it?'

He smiled and opened his college bag, pulling out two bottles of beer with a notorious grin on his face.

'*Abey ye kahan se kharida?* How did you get this?' I asked, inquisitive.

'From the market,' he said matter of factly.

'But it's hot. I think beers are enjoyed when chilled.'

'You are right,' he said and asked me to put the bottles in the common hostel refrigerator.

I was obviously reluctant to do so. And since he sounded so cool and pretty daring, I asked him to do it instead. 'Why don't you go! You are brave. I fear being caught by the warden.'

'Come on, don't be such a baby. We are in second year now,' he replied.

Ultimately, I did not go and had the beer warm. But all in all, my second year at college did not go so well. Having adjusted to college life, I took things more casually and even began skipping classes. The teachers were friendly with the students and did not seem concerned. Back home, Fua was getting along fine, so it seemed I could take things a bit easier.

My downfall started when my friends and I began staying up late at night, exchanging gossip and smoking cigarettes. I was still fairly depressed over the loss of Baba and Papa, and initially I used the cigarettes to calm my mind. And within a few months, I found myself addicted.

As an obvious consequence, I tried alcohol and discovered my love for beer. I have said many times, alcohol may not be the solution to any of your problems, but it lets you forget the problem for some time. I wanted to forget everything that had happened to unsettle my life.

At that juncture in life, I needed encouragement and love, but it seemed there was none to be found. Alcohol seemed like my only escape from all of this, and by the time I entered third year, my quest for it increased to the point of taking me to the brink of becoming an alcoholic.

Consequently, in the fifth semester, I failed 5 out of 6 papers. When word of this reached home, everyone in my family talked of nothing but my failure. I was so humiliated. This result shook me to my core. It made the thought sink in that after all of my hard work to fulfil Papa's dreams for me, I could lose it all!

I realized that I may fail to graduate unless I reigned myself in and put a check on everything that was responsible for my failing grades. Practically overnight, I stopped sitting up late with friends, and I quit drinking altogether. These sacrifices were rewarded, for in the very next semester, I cleared 11 departmental papers and dodged a bullet – I would not have to stay a year back, after all.

It is worth noting that for all the talk that went on among my family members when I was failing, not a word was said about my success in clearing the papers. It's shameful that people are willing to tear each other down, but so unwilling to build up their loved ones. But this seems to be human nature – negatives are glaringly obvious, but positives are often overlooked.

As the last year of college came to a close, everyone who had not yet been placed into a job was tense, including me. I felt extreme pressure from my family and friends to quality in the campus drive. One mass recruiter came and almost 60% of the students were placed. And still, I was not. This had nothing to do with my studies; placement depends entirely on how well you do in the interviews. Finally, I was able to get placement in my core subject in Maharashtra. I was so grateful to finally move beyond the stress of it all.

❖

The liver makes billirubin.
Bilirubin is formed when the haemoglobin in red cells is broken down. The liver is essential in metabolizing this protein; if bilirubin levels get too high, jaundice results.

भूरा / *Bhura : Brown*

Death can come so suddenly, but even when there is prolonged illness, a family can never be prepared for the loss of a loved one – particularly when that loved one is the bread-winner of the family. Other relatives drifted away from us once the financial support was gone, but my brother and I were missing so much more than just Papa's money. He was not only generous financially; he had set our paths out clearly before us, and his departure left us feeling completely rudderless.

When my own liver disease began years later, I could not help but remember the events of that fateful night, and I found it difficult to remain positive in the face of the same illness that had claimed Papa. I thank god for Disha and her family. Without their encouragement, support and love, I do not know how I would have survived an illness I knew could so easily – and quickly – take a life.

Chapter 4

Love and Marriage

गुलाबी / *Gulabi : Pink*

I shivered slightly on the gurney, as much from nerves as from the chill in the room. One of the attendants pulled a sheet higher onto my chest, then they both turned towards the door.

'Do you have anyone with you?' one of them turned and asked.

'My wife,' I said. 'She is in the waiting room.'

He looked at the other attendant and nodded, then she left the room, apparently to find Disha. 'She can see you now; just keep apart, okay?' the attendant said, as he walked through the door. I nodded. That would not be a problem; we had been informed many times about how important it was to keep everything antiseptic just before surgery.

Disha came into the room and sat on a chair near my gurney. I just looked at her, so grateful for more time together. She looked into my eyes, and this time, I did not see fear. She was composed. All I could see there was love, contentment, acceptance… everything a man could want from a wife.

'I love you, Disha,' I said softly.

'I love you too,' she said and smiled. There wasn't any need to say more, but we made idle conversation to pass the time.

At one point, while she was talking, I looked up at the ceiling. 'What a woman,' I thought. She had taken me places I never knew, both spiritually and otherwise. As she continued to share the latest news, reading from her phone, my mind drifted. Trying to keep my nerves from getting the best of me, I began to reflect on the day we met, and our life together ever since.

❖

4.1. Adolescence

'Ashu?'

Fua was calling me from the kitchen, but I was too distracted to hear her. She leaned her head to the doorway and called again.

'Ashu!'

That time I heard her. I looked up from my phone. 'Yes, Fua?'

'Ashu, why do you not answer when I call you?' She seemed a bit impatient, so I tried to make myself look as innocent as possible.

'I'm deeply sorry, Fua. What can I do for you?'

'Ashu, someday you will have a wife who will call out your name a hundred times. This is good practice for you, if you listen to me now.'

'Yes, Fua,' I replied, knowing there was no use in trying to argue with her. I looked at her shoes, waiting for her to tell me what was needed.

'Let the boy be...' It was Baba speaking from the kitchen table. I could always count on *Baba* to stand up for me.

'Well, someday...' Fua started, then trailed off in deference to him.

I was a light-hearted kid, who loved games and toys. Growing up and having a family was the last thing on my mind, and Baba knew that. He was in no hurry to see me grow up; he knew that life requires that of each of us all too soon.

'Ashu...' Baba called out from the kitchen.

'Yes, Baba?' I answered.

'Please come to me,' he said, and I scrambled to my feet. When I bounced into the kitchen, he gave me his generous smile and said, 'Sit here!'

I took the chair next to him. My legs had grown just long enough to reach the floor. Being able to touch the ground with my toes gave me a proud feeling, like maybe I had grown up a bit, even if Fua didn't think so.

'Ashu, your Fua is right about something,' Baba began, and somehow I knew what he was saying was important, even though he had a laugh in his voice. 'Some day you will be a man, and this is a very different thing from being a boy.'

'Yes, Baba,' I responded, though I had no idea what he meant. I knew men were men and boys were boys, but other than being taller and having a deeper voice, they seemed the same to me, though maybe more tired.

'You're a good boy, Ashu,' Baba began again, 'but we all want you to grow up to be a good man.'

I nodded. 'Do you know what a good man does?' he asked.

I looked at the walls, then at the ceiling, waiting to see if he would tell me. Baba remained silent, so I started to try to think of an answer. 'Ahh… he takes care of children?' I guessed. That is what Baba did for me, and I knew he was a good man.

'Yes, yes,' Baba agreed. 'Indeed. A good man always takes care of children. What else?'

'Umm…' I hesitated, knowing Fua was within earshot. I lowered my voice, 'And women?' I knew Baba did a lot to help Fua too – and not just with the housework.

Baba chuckled. 'Sure, sure,' he said. 'Women too. But there is something more important.'

I started drawing a square on the table. I had no idea what else to say. I knew if I delayed long enough, Baba would tell me the right answer. Finally he drew in a breath, and I thought he would speak again, but instead he reached over and picked up an apple and started eating it. I paused in my square-drawing, looking up at his face to see if he was still waiting for me to answer, but I could not tell.

After a moment more, Baba shifted in his seat and looked past Fua, out the window. I followed his glance. Outside, I could see the sun shining between the trees. People were passing by, some just wandering, but others with purpose, as if they had somewhere to be.

'Baba,' I started hesitantly. 'What else does a good man do?'

'Oh, Ashu,' he said, 'we're doing it.' Then he laughed his hearty laugh. I laughed too. For me it was just a game. 'Go back to your phone, you silly boy,' he said, ruffling my hair with his hand. I bounced happily back to the chair in the other room, picked up my phone, and started playing again.

❖

4.2 Introduction with Disha

My earlier fiasco in the interview with a company didn't dampen my yearning for a great job, and trying again soon. My fingers slipped as I tried to button my shirt; the buttons just didn't seem to want to go through the holes. I looked up at my face in the mirror. 'You look too nervous,' I told myself. Turmoil of my last face to face round kept me dubitable of clearing this round. I must have come across as a naive developer lacking even the basics of programming last time when they interviewed me. I was a newbie in software development, and a transition in my domain from software testing to software development made things even worse. But that was one year back, and now I was looking at changing my domain. I was now amongst star performer in my current company. I have been working so hard to enhance my skills and there was scarcely any situation where I would roll on my task to a more proficient professional. Bygone were the days when my nerves got the best of me whenever I was encountered with questions. I was sure I was a changed guy now.

'Look at the time, Ashu. You were supposed to reach for the interview by now,' my mother said in a shrill voice from the kitchen.

I looked at the glinting digits of watch fastened on my wrist. I recently was awarded EOM (employee of the month) and this was my gift. It showed 10:30 a.m.

'Still have some time to spare, Maa. The place is just ten minutes away,' I replied.

'Why do you always leave things for the last hour,' she shrieked.

'Breakfast is set on the table. I have made your favourite pooris. Please don't go on an empty stomach again. And don't even think of leaving it uneaten. It takes a lot of vigorous attempts to earn your bread and butter, so acknowledge that,' she screamed.

It was more of a routine for my mother to yell at me to have my breakfast, which I would usually skip as I was mostly in a hurry.

I grabbed a poori from the table, rolled it with some aloo sabji and gobbled it down with gulps of water. Before long, I got into my car, still chewing the other poori my mother had stuffed into my mouth as I was leaving.

After some security checks, I was finally allowed to get into the FSG facility. As I made my way into the company, it made me smile. Damn it! This place was amazing. The dull yellow from the outside of the building didn't carry on into the inside. The walls were grey, and the crown moulding was white. The baseboards were red. Even the tiled floors had a bright tint to them. To my left was the conference room, with a bright blue accent wall where the television was mounted against its surface. To my right was a hallway, with the light blue carrying all the way down its expanse toward a metro gate at the end of it that carried to the workstations.

They had also pinned the company's core values along a wall, but I did not bother to reflect on any and check whether any of them were instilled in me. All that said, I was enthralled by the splendour of the place. I could just envisage what a privilege it would be for me to be working here.

Despite preparing so hard, I couldn't stop my feet from trembling when an HR came and asked for my CV, replacing it with a form that carried all the basic details. Unlike other times, I didn't borrow a pen from someone as I was carrying one, and started filling the form. My face dug into the form, I could hardly catch anything going around, when I was interrupted by a girl intruding into and dissolving my attention.

'Hi, could you please lend me your pen?' she asked very gently.

Her voice was so pleasing that I couldn't resist looking up. I could only gaze at her in astonishment. It was a long time since a beautiful girl was seeking a favour from me. Not withstanding the fact that I was still filling in the form, I handed over my pen to her.

A soft thanks with a smile could suffice and was like water to my desolated heart. I could feel my heart pounding already. She took a seat next to me and I could not hold back to steal frequent glances while she was filling her form. Before long, my name was announced. My mind was swirling, seeking for an opportunity to talk to her.

'Ashu... you're next,' announced the HR. Even two rounds of announcements were not enough to stir me from the fantasy my mind was weaving with the girl I just saw.

'Yes sir,' I replied hurriedly.

'Please follow me.' I tailgated him till we reached a conference room where a panel of experts were already reviewing my form.

'Please take a seat,' he said handing my CV to one of the members of the interview panel.

Five members to thump my brain with questions! Is it an interview to recruit a scientist, I thought? I never expected so many members in the panel and it was freaking me out.

'Hi Ashu! I am Manas, the director, GS Noida. Please brief us about yourself.' One of them asked while still turning over the pages of my CV. He was a fair, stout, middle-aged man, completely bald and clean shaved.

Memories of my previous rejection made me uneasy. I had to be very careful with my answers. He wasn't from a technical panel though, but the sovereignty of decision to recruit or reject remained with him.

I was interrupted in the middle of my answer by a relatively younger recruiter. 'That's fair enough, Ashu. Let's move to some technical stuff. I can see you have been the employee of the month twice in your previous company. Could you please let us know when you best overcame a challenging situation. Emphasize on the problem and your approach.'

I could get into enough trouble had I not primed for it. I answered very well, giving examples of two untoward situations I encountered and provided discrete solutions to.

'Impressive! I quite liked your approach,' he replied.

His motivating words were enough for me to crack on all their subsequent questions.

The last words they said were, 'Wait outside and the HR will connect with you.'

These words were enough for a cue that I was selected. I could not resist a smile and provided them my assurance to work with diligence, while taking my leave from them.

The moment I stepped out of the interview room, I was reminded of that adorable girl I had met. My eyes were still hunting for her glimpse, when I was slightly jolted backward.

'Hey, I had been looking for you to return your pen. How was your interview?'

'I think I did okay. They have asked me to wait. Let's see,' I said.

'How about yours, Miss...?' I questioned deliberately with some uttering, should she wish to fill tell her name while responding.

'Oh , I am Disha. They already selected me. I just came in for some formalities. Glad to know your interview was nice, and I hope I see you on the floors,...' she replied.

'Ashu,' I completed her sentence. 'For that to happen, I must clear the next round, though,' I clarified.

'Come on! Everyone knows what the HR round is all about. If you are not aspiring for a hike of more than 40 percent, you are certainly in.' I merely smiled, while she sniggered, 'Are you looking for more?'

I still could not say anything, and she further said, 'I will take your leave now. Will catch you later, if at all you compromise with your aspirations of uneven salary hike. Best of luck!'

She was of medium height and quite fair. The black sleeveless top and skinny jeans made her look very pretty. Glossy red highlighter adorned her sleek brown hair that rebounded as she walked and a thin golden necklace perfectly ran into her cleavage. A small conversation with her left me thinking of ways to talk to her again soon.

The HR recruiter put simpler questions about my previous organization and purpose for job change. They didn't bother to ask more on my profile, but they remained very strict in salary negotiation and tried to cut on any rise on my demands. I flashed a winning smile while shaking hands and bidding goodbyes to the recruiter. Success in the interview kept me smiling throughout the day.

The next morning, I hustled to work, not wanting to be listed as a late comer. Preoccupied and anxious at the thoughts of resigning, I reached my office dot on time. I had worked here for a while and valued my personal relationship with my colleagues to an extent that I thought of seeking a prior discussion before I could put in my papers.

I was sitting on my chair, my head buried in my hands, pretty anxious. I was worried about the reaction of my manager over my resignation, until he nudged me to know the matter.

I revealed to him that I wanted to move forward in my career. I shared with him how much I was engrossed with the grandeur of the office I was selected for and enthusiasm of grabbing a new opportunity laid down for me ahead. I was wondering whether I should post my resignation on the portal. It was a shock for him, as the team was dependent on me. Losing me would be a setback for them, but he was aware of the splendour and fame of the company I had been selected for. He already knew retaining me would not work even with a high salary offer. But even then he suggested that I rethink once before declaring my resignation on the portal.

Two months of notice won't suffice for a proper substitute, but I had been remarkably steadfast and persevering. They could rely on me to clear all stacked issues of ongoing projects. Two months of notice period passed in a flash and now it was time to say my final adieus.

From: ashu@nucleus.com
To: finnone_dev@nucleus.com
Greetings everyone!

It has been a while working with you all, but now I have sought a better opportunity and have decided to move forward in my career. During the last three years of my career, you all have provided me support and through your encouragement and guidance, I have been able to excel at all the projects offered to me. With many of you, I have shared a unique camaraderie which I hope will continue in the years to come, even though I shall not be here with the company. I now look forward to a new position that brings forth new challenges and adds more diverse experience to my career.

I do wish you and the company every success in all its future endeavours.

Thanks and regards,

Ashu

The moment I sent my last words to my team, I found myself much at ease. Anxiety of the future was replaced by fantasies of Disha. She said she was working in Cyber City Gurgaon, but I could only find dismalness. It was very difficult to spot her in the crowd that assembled around the common area every time the office was dismissed.

❖

'**Success is counted the sweetest.**'

These words by Emily Dickinson are very true reflection of human behaviour. Until we savour success, we remain unware of its tanginess. But with every success we count, we become more desperate to achieve yet another, unaware of what success truly is. Being a fresh graduate, we only understand the pleasure of being employed in a top-notch company with a high salary. We don't understand in that moment that there is still a lot to achieve. Our everlasting desire of success has no ends and we always strive to achieve a still better life, compromising with a whole lot. We cut short on the everything – family, relations, our passions, friends and so much else to provide for our fight for constantly changing success.

We all run after worldly matters which comfort us. But to be truly happy in life, we have to spare some time for our self. We have to learn to live every moment of our life. We have to count our blessings. Not just this, our behaviour and thoughts towards others will give us immense happiness too.

We need to be more contented in our life only then we could be happy. Let's not stop trying for more happiness and success, but let us learn to balance our life well. We should strive for a better me along with a better life.

❖

4.3 On board

On 7 July 2016, I got up as early as the sun to welcome yet another day. I was overwhelmed with enthusiasm to go on board in the new company. The HR person greeted me with warmth and snugness as she ushered me to a room where they finished all the joining formalities and issued me the essentials – bank account, access card, laptop, mobile phone. Induction sessions were organized later to cover the different policies within the company. I found all the sessions really dull and monotonous, with the only exception of a session that elaborated about the Work from Home (WFH) policies and other leave benefits. I was enthralled to know the flexibility provided to the employees. I was really amused by their WFH policy. I have seen many of my friends take pride in talking about it. I always thought any such policy is predominantly a prerogative of very limited number of employees placed in top-notch companies. I was really happy to be here.

While the session was still in progress, I heard my name being announced by the HR person peeking from outside. 'Ashu , please catch up with your manager. He has been looking for you for a while. Make sure you return to the sessions after you are done. It's mandatory to attend all the sessions and we will continue with it for the next three days. Then you should join your team, and this applies to everyone,' he announced.

I made an exit from the room to a lounge where the same gentleman who interviewed me and was really impressed with my answer was sitting. He was accompanied by another colleague. 'Hey Ashu! I am Punit. Welcome on board. I am glad you joined. Once you complete your sessions, please come directly to the 8th floor. We have planned a boot camp training for all the new joinees in Gurgaon, which will start from the coming Monday. I will be your reporting manager, looking at the operational stuffs. We all are working independently for a client and scrum masters are our technical manager. You would learn about the processes gradually, once you acquaint yourself with the new environment.'

'Hi Punit! Thanks for the heads up and sorting out the plan so nicely. Can I please have your number, just in case I need to call you.'

With that, I resumed with the sessions that continued for three days before we actually went on board and amalgamated with my team.

Punit presented me formally to the team that was ramified throughout DNA (the root). My expertise best matched the integration team. It took a while for me to meet the whole team.

While getting introduced, my gaze cheated to scan the room beyond, hoping to find a glimpse of Disha.

'Hey Ashu.' I heard someone calling as I made my way back to Punit. I approached the young man sheepishly.

'Hi, I'm Shivam. I have been assigned as your peer, to help you in case of any issues. You can connect with me if you have any problem dealing with IT, HR or even the client. I will help you with the process and will guide you through all the service portals. You are required to shadow me to learn the processes and standards we follow in our coding. You can pull out a chair and sit with me until you get your machine and work station.' He was polite and confident.

'Hi Shivam! So nice of you to offer a seat. I was just beginning to wonder where I go from here.'

He seemed to be an affable companion. Apart from untangling the various concepts and processes followed in company, he also talked on personal stuff.

'Do you know Disha?' I asked abruptly interjecting him in the middle of our conversation. I realised I was comfortable enough with him to do that.

He turned around on his chair with a question mark expression pasted on his face. 'I hardly know any girls named Disha. Are you talking about someone in our team?' he almost chuckled at my expression and anxiety, I guess.

'I presumed you already knew her, Shivam bhai. I met her during our interview. She must be in our team if she joined the company.'

'Let me check from the employee directory,' he said with a smile and swirled his chair around again to face his laptop.

He punched in Disha's name on the office messenger to get the list of all the employees named Disha. It divulged a handful of employees, which on filtering on the basis of project, revealed the one I was looking for.

'Seat no – 8057,' Shivam announced. Before long, I stood up to gawk at every girl on the floor, to catch a glimpse of Disha.

'She is offline since yesterday. Seems like she is on leave. You can run across her on Monday. If you wish, I can assign her to upskill you. I just need to take consent from Punit which I am sure would be an easy clinch,' Shivam propounded.

How nice of him, I thought, I couldn't cease to appreciate and thanks Shivam for the rest of the day. Punit had, in the meantime, already scheduled the boot camp training at client location in Gurgaon from next week. Looking at the cab details of the training, I was further enchanted when I saw Disha as my co-rider. It must be Shivam, I thought.

Daily commute from Noida to Gurgaon was a little less weary with Disha. We talked about the training, laughed at the trainers sometimes, but hardly bothered about the assessment. The trainers had made clear from day one that only those who cleared the evaluation at the end of the training would be allowed to continue in the project. Our training would start at 8 a.m. and last till 4 p.m. The urge to meet Disha kept me going. I spoke to her, sent her carefully selected WhatsApp messages, but the irony of the situation was that I expected her to understand my feelings but hesitated to express it.

Even a month later, I could not express my feelings to her for the fear of rejection. But now I was determined to tell her. I felt I had earned some place in her heart. I wondered why else would she reciprocate on my messages and love quotes. So, I decided to call her for a date.

'Hello Disha... Listen, would you mind accompanying me for dinner tomorrow?' I asked sheepishly.

'Come again! Did I hear you asking me out for a date? It sounds fishy to me.' She giggled.

'No... no! I thought of meeting you on my birthday,' I lied.

'Is it! That's cool then. Let us catch up tomorrow. WhatsApp me the venue details and I will be there.'

I was exhilarated. I lied to her, but so what! The most important thing here was that I would be out on a date with her. I had to share it with someone! Shivam.

That December Sunday, I picked up my clothes carefully. I tried so many things from my wardrobe, but eventually decided to wear narrow fit jeans with a simple white shirt, wrapped beneath a stylish Korean jacket to resist the nip in the air. I reached the mall in Noida well before time and waited for Disha to join in a restaurant on the top floor. I ordered some starters and sat there, anxiously waiting. I saw her coming from the glass boundary of the restaurant. She was wearing a sleeveless top and skirt. Her jacket hung on her slim curves and her sleek and brown hair was adorned by a glossy red highlighter which fluttered while she walked. My gaze lingered on her lips as she walked towards me.

'Hey Ashu! What's the plan?' she asked as she sat down opposite me.

'No plan, Disha. I just called you to talk. Umm, and I lied to you about my birthday. I could have spoken to you over phone, but then I thought, I must tell you what I feel for you eye to eye. I have imagined opening my heart to you umpteen times in my dreams. Maybe it is time to do it in person too.' I explained straight away.

'I already knew it's not your birthday. We are connected on Facebook, remember? So I know it's two months away. I came here because you pressed so much. Now that I have come, please tell why you called me so imminently.'

'Wow, okay! But please don't cut me in between, while I speak. Please.'

She nodded and I started talking. 'Ever since I saw you, my mind is flooded with your thoughts. When you left that day after the interview, the urge to run into you was so intense that to catch glimpse of you, I didn't hesitate to trespass into Cyber City innumerable times. But it was all in vain. Later, on joining FSG first thing I asked in the team was if you had joined. My love for you is so deep that everything I look at, seems to be your reflection. Quite unlike my usual self, I was never tempted to take time off during the entire training session because I didn't want to lose any chance to see you. I am so very desperate to have you in my life, Disha. Please don't belittle my love… at least give me a chance. I will love you the most and will do anything for you please… please.'

I pulled out a bouquet of roses from my bag pack and went down on my knees right beside her. 'I love you, Disha. Please give me a chance. I'll love you like no other; I will never hurt you, I promise.'

Disha couldn't speak much except muttering a few things I could not understand. I could not make out whether she was snorting or moved by my words. When I saw her unmoved for a while, I walked over to her. I set my hand on her shoulder and turned her around to face me. I put my hand beneath her chin and tilted it up. Her eyes met mine and I gazed into the beautiful orbs.

I wondered if I could kiss her. I could make out she would not stop me. But I ceased my temptation. I took her hand in mine and said, 'Disha, no matter what you decide, I promise we shall be friends.'

She blinked.

❖

'Take the first step in faith. You don't have to see the whole staircase, just take the first step.'

—Martin Luther king jr.

Each one of has aspirations, but the moment we find it perilous, are we not hesitant to take even the first step? We lose faith very easily sometimes and it shows in different events of our life. Is it not true even when our life is going on well, that we fear for our future. Irrespective of our bright present, we worry about securing an even brighter future.

But you know what, every negative thought is like a virus in our life that depletes our energy to perform well. We must have faith in our goals and only then we can bring it to realization.

Had I not taken a chance to speak to Disha – despite the fear that she could stop talking to me – I would have remained indifferent to her love. We can never know what future holds for us, but the best we can do is live in the present and strive to make it the second to none moment of our life. Our efforts in unison with our beliefs will work wonders. That is when every object of the universe will start shedding energy for us and conspire with us to work magic in our life. Fearing a future will only mess with our present.

❖

4.4 My Advent on new life

My mind still lingered on what had happened that day. Sitting on a chair, right beside my window, I was gazing at the cars passing through the driveway. My brain was still reeling in the multiple thoughts –Would she ever call me? Why did I open my heart to her so soon? It could end up our relationship even as friends!

My mind was flooded with the remorse of proposing to Disha, until I heard my phone ringing. It was Disha calling. I had customized my ringtone to differentiate her calls, so I knew the moment it rang. I literally jumped up to answer her call.

'Hello Ashu! Why are you not coming to the office? Punit and Shivam were asking for you. Are you not well?'

Okay, so she was feigning indifference to what all had happened between us the other day. I didn't want to pull the same strings by talking about it any further, not yet. I didn't want our relationship to be estranged. If I reiterate, she might stop calling me forever… like the past few days.

'Hi Disha! So nice to hear from you. I am doing fine yaar. Sorry about disappearing. I will join back from tomorrow.'

'Great! I had been missing your scrumptious thekua from your lunch. Tell aunty to prepare some more. I would take back few for my home.'

'Sure will.'

I hadn't been answering any calls in the last three days. I would just text them, 'I'm not available'. Disha's call had livened me up and I was back at work the very next day. Our in-house training had commenced, and Disha had joined before me. She was well aquatinted with the processes being followed within the company. Punit assigned her to train me, in lieu of Shivam.

Later that evening, I saw Disha in the office cafeteria.

'Hi Disha! Can I join you?'

'Come on, Ashu! Why are you being so formal? Friends need not ask.'

'I thought you were not very happy with what I did the other day, so i was just playing formal, to be on the safer side,' I told her honestly.

'I wasn't unhappy or anything; it's just that I wasn't prepared for things alternating at such a pace. I have always counted you as a friend. I think we should give time to our relationship before we actually get into commitment. We should earn each other's trust.'

That was like the light at the end of the tunnel, and I was prepared to go through the dark for it.

I was now geared up to join the project. Two months of training had prepared me to counter the requirements of the client independently. Today was the first time I would take part in scrum call and the client would assign me an item. I had to be the best in delivering.

'Hey everyone, my name is Rishabh. Let's have one round of formal introduction, before I actually assign work items to you all.'

I was procured for a new project, but to measure my diligence, Rishabh had assigned me a maintenance item first.

The item assigned to me was as easy as a pie; it just required a one-liner change. I wondered why Rishabh has assigned such an easy task to me. Perhaps he wanted to check my acquaintance with the processes being followed. Not thinking on it more than that, I checked in my changes.

Rishabh was from the client side working in the USA. I had struggled with him in the initial days, when the project was very demanding, but later we gelled up well. I would always seek him for the due motivation and encouragement which I owed from other peers in the Noida facility. I never met with him face to face, but I could always count him as a friend more than just a peer. I worked with him day and night to realize the deadline of some of the critical projects sometimes.

'Hi Ashu! Congratulations on your first check in. I'm glad you have done it well before time. Let's now manifest the same expertise on a broader scale on the new requirements.'

Rishabh allocated me tasks of the new project. I was among the few new joiners to be designated to work in projects and its requirements from the very inception, while others were still assigned maintenance of the running projects. I started on it well and was contended with that.

My 'friendship' with Disha was going well. I would always seek her advice before implementing anything both professionally and personally. She would always extend her support beyond the ambit of her professional limits. She turned out to be the friend I would trust for anything. I never hesitated to speak up to her about anything in my life, and we would often be at either her place or mine for long gossips. She stayed with her friends in a paying guest accommodation in Noida.

I landed into her apartment without notifying her beforehand one day. I presumed she would have said a clear no if I had asked for her prior permission that day. That's because she was alone in the house, and I did not know that. Her flatmates were away. I only figured I had earned her trust when she let me in and welcomed me with a grin.

'Such odd timing, Ashu. No one is in the flat.'

'Is it really odd! I would rather count it as bliss in disguise.' I murmured. When I saw her staring at me, I said out loud, 'No worries. I had just bought some chicken for you, you had been telling me all these days that you wished to eat home style chicken cooked by me.'

'Oooo, so nice of you Ashu, but....'

'Do you not feel safe with me?'

'Nothing like that, Ashu. I trust you and that's why you're standing inside the house, even when I am all by myself.'

'That answers your question Disha. If you trust me, allow me.'

Quietly we sneaked to her kitchen. Disha feared her neighbours would learn of my presence and create a ruckus. We both danced in the kitchen to find the pan and other kitchen tong before I could start cooking. Disha went back to her room once I started to cook. The plumes of the scrumptious flavour of the food enticed her to the kitchen again. Quietly she sneaked into the kitchen behind me; I was turning food in a pan.

As she touched my shoulder, she leaned close to my ear and whispered, 'You are amazing.'

'I know already dear,' I said simply, feigning indifference to her words. 'Now set the table.'

Before she could begin to express mock disappointment at my lack of reaction, I turned to her. I looked deeply into those bright emerald eyes glistened as a smile crossed her face. Her nose crinkled softly, and I tried my best to quell the traitorous flutter in my chest. I was not mistaken – I could feel love for me brimming in her eyes. I gently squeezed her shoulders to steal a small kiss from her neck.

She rolled her eyes in exasperation. But before she could react, I put a large spoon full of yummy chicken into her mouth.

Her expression changed. 'It's so delicious, Ashu.'

She was so lost in the delectable treat that she overlooked my mischief. She started walking away from me towards the hall to set the table. She brushed past me, and the fragrance of her perfume dragged me towards her. I watched her hair billow back. Her top waved remarkably over her soft curves and her jeans clung to her legs, I tried my best not to stare at the swaying of her hips.

'Very nice Ashu. I must take some training from you. It tastes great,' she said again. We ate together and I had never felt so complete.

I thanked Disha for the wonderful evening before leaving her house that night.

In office the next day, I was wrestling with my work items. Rishabh was very particular about the coding. He focused on the micros to find out where I had gone wrong. Mere coding to meet the functionality didn't work with him.

He would send meeting invites randomly, to discuss the impediments of any ongoing task assigned to me. These were done often at the spur of the moment, without much prior discussions.

'Hey Ashu, sorry about setting up a meeting so late, but we are already lagging in the project. To avoid chaos down the line, I want to wrap things up at full tilt,' he started.

'Not an issue Rishabh, I'm fine on that. Let's talk in ten minutes.'

'I saw your changes, but I am not sure whether you did some impact analysis, I also feel it could be coded more efficiently. There are too many variable declaration and discrete conditional statements in your code. Try some alternative way to reduce the use of variables and merge the different conditional statements in your code. But we need to be fast to implement the changes.

'Don't you feel it's bit irrational Rishabh? I mean, you are accusing my code of not meeting up the standards, and at the same time, you are grilling me on time. I am ready for any changes, but I would require an effort estimation before I can commit for the changes,' was all I could say.

'It's perfectly fine. Will reconvene the discussion in a day, when you are done with the changes.'

Clients can be tough at times, irrespective of whatever you feel. They need everything done in a jiffy. I called Disha to discuss everything that has happened.

'Hey Disha, this man Rishabh is very annoying… the most vexing person I have ever met. In spite of my code working properly, he wants me to take a holistic approach in my coding. What a freak!'

'Cool down, Ashu! Many times in life we find people behave contrary to our expectations. Let us not be so quick to judge him. He might be under some stress with things moving a bit differently. You cannot make everyone behave as per your presumption and this perhaps is the beauty of life. Is it necessary that I will think the same me as you, if he feels this needs to be changed and has some potential reasons for it. I think you should change it on forefront. I'm sure you will earn his trust gradually and will make a very strong bond with him in due course of time. Do as he says, don't be loath to adapt the changes.'

'Irrespective of what you say Disha, I need to finish it even if I am reluctant to recode.'

'Great, I am glad you are doing it. And listen, if you are working on it anyway, why not work on it with enthusiasm? Why be caught up in reluctance and doubts?'

'I never knew you were such a mentor, Disha. Thanks for your help. I will certainly draw some benefits from you in near future.

❖

'Earning trust'

Trust is very brittle; it takes years of hard work and commitment to build, and once it's built, it takes even more to carry on with it. It's a value which is reflected in different events of our life: professional or personal, or both together.

Do we ever think what is the reason of an organisation having innumerable satisfied clients while others not. It's trust playing its role. It can be easy to coax a client by false commitments and flattering, but to have them stay for long, we need to build trust.

Let's understand it better. Assume you go to a fruit market to buy apples. You find all the vendors selling it on same rate; the quality of the fruit is also the same everywhere. What would be a discriminating factor that helps you decide on a vendor? The one who is gentle in behaviour may coax you to buy from him at first, but the one who refrains from giving you apples with a humble submission that his apples are not fresh and gives you an option to buy another fruit earns your trust. You may not buy apples from him today, but next time, you will surely find him for buying apples and also recommend him to all your friends.

❖

4.5 Drawing near

Me: *Dishu, movie tonight?*

Disha: *Hmm... might turn problematic at night, better plan out something in the morning. Delhi is insecure to wander at night.*

Me: *Fine jaan, we can sketch out something tomorrow morning. I am sure you will plan out something in the spur of the moment from your whimsical mind.*

Disha: *No way, I won't bunk office for your imbecilic plans. Wait till Saturday……*

Me: *Not again…*

The floodgates opened and we ended up chatting about everything. Our conversation morphed from formal chit-chat to more vivid gossip, sometimes carrying reminiscences of past. I could correlate with all her struggle as a teenager to compete for the engineering test. Any such talks would remind me of my early days as a child in a small town, trying hard to draw some light to study from the traditional lantern that burned kerosene to produce some light. I could only wonder how Disha had managed to crack this vying examination from a small town with meagre support.

I had to wait for an entire week for our first date. This was for the first time we were going out for a movie. I cranked the engine of the Bullet I had borrowed from Shivam. Being a teenager, I always dreamt about a girl riding pillion. With Disha, my dream was coming true.

The roar of the motorcycles reverberated all along my jaunt. Disha was already there when I landed up at the mall, waiting in the food court.

She was looking down at the porch of the building holding the rails of the boundary when I caught a glimpse of her. My god, she looked ravishing in the traditional dress she wore – a sleeveless suit with deep V cut neck adorned by a fine chain. Sleek bracelet wrapped on her wrist, the mascara was prominent on her bright emerald eyes that glistened. Crimson lipstick smeared on her lips that perfected her nail paint.

I emerged before her suddenly, while her eyes were still fixed on the porch of the building. I nudged her from behind her.

'Hi beautiful!'

She never had a hint of me appearing so suddenly. She looked completely nonplussed and bewildered hearing someone greeting her until she turned back to see it was me.

'Can you not run down your surprises a bit?' she scowled.

'Ok ok, I am sorry honey. So what's the plan?'

'You coaxed me into coming, you figure out something,' she said mocking.

'I leave it to your whims, Dishu. I am open to whatever you plan, although I think we should go for a movie.'

'Fine, let's not waste time then.'

We were jostled by the pushing of the crowd rushing towards the entrance. It was a packed house and all my dreams of chit chatting with her were gone. I tried to kiss her several times while watching the movie, but she restrained me from doing so. Although she held my hand throughout the movie. After the movie, we headed to a restaurant for lunch. We held the corner most seat of the restaurant, away from the crowd. She sat next to me, all my senses overtaken by her fragrance. I couldn't take it anymore and slipped my hand on her back. She dug her face into my chest and closed her eyes. She lost herself wrapped in my arms. I could only say 'love you Dishu' a thousand times and fold her hair to kiss her. I wanted her close to me so badly that I pulled her to me, tighter than ever. I kissed her as I said 'Love you Dishu' unceasingly.

I wished time could freeze and I could be in her arms till doomsday. When a waiter showed up with our order, we pulled ourselves up in a flash. Disha was still arranging her tousled hair while he kept the order on the table.

'Enjoy your food sir,' he said before leaving.

After that day, we never missed any chance of eating together. We would feed each other as we ate, our habit of sharing food remained alike even during my illness, which was knocking at the doors to blow out our love and wreck our life very soon.

After lunch, I moved to the parking lot with Disha, her hand in mine. I didn't want to leave her, but we had to separate and I had to drop her.

'Hey, you bought a bike! When?' Disha asked surprised.

'Haha, it isn't mine. It is Shivam's. Just to carve a masculine impression on you.' I winked.

'Hmm, had it been your own vehicle, even if smaller, I would have been more pleased.'

'Fine Dishu. Let's go now.'

I rode my bike with her riding pillion. She wrapped her arms over my waist tightly. I could feel her warmth. I drove very slow, yet we reached her flat really fast. As she steeped out from the bike, I felt my heart cease to beat. I felt like I had left my heart with her. I kissed her, she waved at me and tossed kisses to me standing at the porch of her apartment until she could manage to get the glimpse of me as I rode back.

Back in office, things turned favourable for me swiftly. I adopted Disha's approach of dealing with people. I earned Rishabh's trust gradually. Everything was going on very well until I was hit by a untoward situation when one of my codes broke at the client's end.

My phone was ringing at night, and showed Punit calling. Late night call from office was enough as a cue that something unexpected has happened. I got up in a flash and jogged outside of my room to pick his call, not wanting to disturb Maa.

'Ashu, sorry for calling so late. But one of your codes is breaking at client side and it has been escalated highly. You need to fix it immediately. Please pull out your laptop and try and fix it now. Guys in the U.S. are available to help you.'

'Alright sir. If it so urgent, I will try to wrap this up right away,' I said.

Rishabh and other peers from our office were waiting for me to join. Looking at the error, I realized I had missed something that was breaking a particular scenario and it had escaped the QA team too. All things being so messy, none of my peers overlooked the present situation to work for the solution with me. On the contrary, they didn't miss any chance of jeering at me for this miss. Had they sought a solution as soon as we spotted trouble, we would have ended up with a result really fast, which otherwise took three long hours of long and useless discussions.

Next day in office, I saw a message from Manas on my Skype messenger.

'Hello Ashu,

Not overlooking your dismal performance in recent time, with the client and you finding the project a hard nut to crack, we have decided to move you to

Performance Improvement Plan (PIP), wherein your annual appraisal will be restricted and all of your tasks will be monitored until we find you worthy for the project.

Hope you will give it your best shot and come out of this with flying colours.'

It was all fake. I was a victim of professional mockery, when everybody put me in the spot. They couldn't put me on PIP just for one miss. I wrote back to Manas in exasperation.

'Hello Manas,

I doubt whether you are aware of what actually has happened last night. Regardless of that, do you think it is justified to put someone on PIP just for one miss? I think we should discuss this further before we actually implement any such actions, as it could harm my career.'

This was highly unacceptable for me, but the decision was revoked post discussion with the client. I thought the bigwigs in FSG were confined within their cabins in the ambit of their managers. They never paid heed to the associates holding lower ranks.

I was highly discouraged and demoralized with what had happened, but with Disha by my side, I overcame the untoward situation swiftly. I had remembered what she had said – irrespective of what you feel for others, you must always strive for doing the right things, the right way.

Things in office turned to my side gradually as I won the trust of clients. I never faced any oddball from any of the peers after this.

❖

4.6 Marriage

I held my breath waiting for Disha's answer on my proposal. What kept me worried was her parents' permission for our marriage. Would she be able to coax them to approve it. Would Disha retaliate if her parents opposed our marriage? My mind was still weaving all such anxiety-driven thoughts when Disha texted me to come to her home. She said her parents wished to meet me and wanted our marriage to be arranged in a way that it appeared like a traditionally set up arranged marriage. I was thrilled and super excited to meet them.

They were very gentle people. Disha's brother was very understanding and looked very composed and contemplative. He asked about my family in a pursuit to find a person who would talk on my behalf. It gave me a whopping hand when I talked about my brother; he knew him already. Things turned in my favour, both on a professional and personal scale, and I was really ecstatic about it… unaware that this happiness was very brief.

My parents had already arranged the marriages of my brother and both of my sisters, so I had some idea of how things would proceed. First the arrangements had to be agreed upon. Both families had met to discuss expenses and how those would be handled, including the dowry.

The controversy of dowry in India is well-known; I do not need to delve too deeply into this subject here. Suffice it to say, sometimes it is not an issue and other times it can go completely out of hands.

Initially, a dowry was intended to help a new wife financially as she adjusted to all of the circumstances of her husband's family. Over the years, however, this custom has grown into a complicated tradition – one sometimes filled with overblown expectations on the groom's side.

When I was a child, my oldest sister married and the groom's family was reasonable. Hers was a love cum arranged marriage, and it proceeded calmly and serenely, with no additional demands beyond what was originally agreed upon.

This was not the case with my younger sister, though. She was in management school at the time, and the demands from the groom's side seemed endless. My father had already passed away, and the financial position of my family was made clear to them, but the groom's relatives insisted on one increase after another. Maa was beside herself the entire time, frustrated with them as they made demands in a most disrespectful way – and eventually she had to take out a loan just to cover the expenses.

It is my sincere hope to see a drastic change in this situation someday. In today's times, where the bride is often as well-educated and financially stable as the groom, there simply is no rationale for the bride's family to be subjected to arbitrary demands from the groom's side. Perhaps someday soon, the families of both sides will contribute equally to the marriage, with neither side assuming a position of supremacy.

Believing as I do now, I do carry some guilt over the demands my family made in arranging my marriage to Disha. Her family raised an independent and successful woman. In spite of her humble beginnings, she managed to get a good education and start a career successfully. Yet my family felt obligated to require her family to meet specific demands in the dowry, and I am sure those demands at times seemed arbitrary and unnecessary to them as well. At the time I thought little of it; I was young and knew no better. Someday, however, I hope I can find a way to make marriage arrangements more equitable.

Once the arrangements had been made, it was time for our families to meet. As we approached the building where her family was staying, I tried my best to appear confident and composed. Secretly, I was breathless with anticipation. My mind raced with all of the questions that were obvious in this situation: Would our families like each other? Would my family like Disha?

We entered the room where her family was waiting, and Disha approached me exactly as she was expected to.

'Disha, this is Fua.' My voice took on a gentle quality, as though I was presenting my own beloved wife to her.

She bowed her head, doing her best not to let her nerves show. 'Hello, Fua. I'm Disha,' she said in the most grown up voice she could muster.

'Hello, Disha,' Fua answered. 'It is good to meet you.' Disha appeared composed, which immediately gave me some admiration for her. After all, she was in the same boat as me, and she likely was just as nervous. I was impressed with her poise.

Around us, our family members were beginning to exchange greetings as they enveloped us. As the sound of all the voices grew louder, I leaned toward Disha.

'You look nice,' I said. And she did. She was wearing a very nice dress with traditional touches to her hair and makeup.

'You do, too,' she responded, but the noise level had grown even louder.

'What?' I asked, leaning closer so that I could hear. She raised her head, speaking directly into my ear.

'I said, you look nice too. I like your tie.'

It was an awkward exchange, this brief formal interaction, but sufficient for the circumstances. We continued to make small talk up to and after the brief ritual where we each committed ourselves to a future together.

On the other hand, for Disha things moved very swiftly in her favour professionally. She got an opportunity in another company, higher salary and higher responsibility. Grabbing this opportunity would even get her an onsite opportunity. I was extremely happy for her.

As our marriage date approached, our trust in one another grew steadily. The wedding was a traditional celebration, with all of the rituals and observances that go along with that. With the little money we had remaining, Disha and I took a public bus 250 kilometres from Delhi to honeymoon at a resort in Mussoorie – a beautiful place in the Himalayan foothills with lovely waterfalls. We had a wonderful time engaging in white water rafting and other adventure sports. I had the best time of my life with her. But little did we know this would be the last time I could do such activities!

We had hoped to stay an entire week in Mussoorie, but Disha received a call from her office after a few days. They had opened a new facility in Pune, and they needed her to visit there. So we both headed to Pune from Mussoorie. While we were in Pune, they announced that Disha had been given a promotion. She was not the manager. I felt so proud of her, and I felt I was a lucky man to have married someone so appreciated by her company.

❖

'Welcome, Disha!' Fua escorted us in from the taxi. We had just returned from Pune, and it was Disha's first time in our household as my bride, though earlier she had been welcomed in our parental house as a part of marriage ritual.

'Thank you, Fua,' Disha replied, tilting her head slightly.

'It is good to be home,' I said. And I meant it. Travelling can be fun, but coming home is always a relief. I took a seat at the kitchen table, while Fua gave Disha a more thorough tour of the house, showing her to what would be our bedroom.

I scrolled on my phone, but something in the back of my mind was asking for attention. I hesitated and looked out of the window. The sun was shining through the trees. People were passing by. It was the same as every other day, but something was different.

I got up and went to pull some cold water bottles from the refrigerator, puzzled over what the difference could be. Just then, Fua and Disha came back into the kitchen. I offered each of them water, which they accepted, opened and began drinking without a break in their conversation. I sat back down at the table, listening and joining in.

Disha was embraced by the whole extended family just as easily, which was a radical adjustment for her. Our backgrounds are quite different. But being the vibrant and adaptable woman she is, Disha managed the change very well. In no time, she was interacting comfortably with everyone and they were warming up to her.

Of all the pleasant surprises Disha had brought into our marriage, one of the best for me has been to see how respectfully she approaches my Fua. Fua, as I have said, had a very difficult life, and by the time Disha entered our family, her asthma was worsening and her health was beginning to fail. Disha approached her like a good daughter who wanted to help her mother, showing Fua deference and taking much care in the household.

My Fua had told me she believed I could lead a very good life with Disha by my side, after she first met her. As I watched Disha so easily become an important part of my family, I quickly came to believe this too. Disha helped me become more organized and responsible. She takes the major credit for bringing me out of pessimism. She consistently encouraged me to maintain positive energy levels.

What followed were days of happiness in which we rejoiced over our life together. My job in IT and Disha's promotion brought in more income, which allowed us to move up in the world. We moved to a large flat and bought a car too. It was fun watching Disha learn to drive!

All seemed right with the world, to me. Together, Disha and I were enjoying life, heedless of the tragedies which were soon to come.

❖

Another important function of the liver is to regulate blood sugar, adding glucose to the blood and taking it away as needed to keep levels consistent.

गुलाबी / *Gulabi : Pink*

Integrating into a new family is already a tremendous challenge for anyone. And more so in one which has put your own family into a difficult position. After the whole presumed dowry situation, I really hoped it was not as difficult for Disha and her family to be comfortable with my family. Even if it was, she was somehow able to stay composed, never for a second showing my family members anything but respect.

If we are blessed to have children, and if it's a boy, there will come a time when I will stand in the groom's family's shoes. That is when the true test of character will come – to see if in my own circumstances I will resist the temptations to make harsh demands or arbitrary requests, or to test the patience of the bride and her family.

With Disha by my side to remind me of the importance of remaining positive, staying organized and making careful decisions, I have no doubt we will handle those arrangements every bit as gracefully as she handled the many changes involved in becoming my wife.

Chapter 5

Heads of Household

पीला / *Peela : Yellow : knowledge and learning; success*

We heard a knock on the door, and two nurses entered the room, wheeling along an IV. We knew it was the anaesthesia, and Disha moved towards the door to make a quick exit if asked. I pretended to pay attention as one of the nurses began explaining what was going to happen. But my thoughts were completely elsewhere, lost in reflection, nervousness, and a strange distance that had taken hold of me, pulling me away from present circumstances like some sort of natural anaesthesia.

As the anaesthesiologist explained the drugs that would be used to keep me sleeping while the doctor operated, I was inevitably reminded of all the hard times... in school, at work, with my family. A part of me wished they could be here to say goodbye, but I knew that was not possible. There was no time.

So often in my life, I felt I had failed them. It's true, I was not always the nephew, son, or brother that I could have been. I could have done better in life. But a part of me wondered why it was Disha's family that had cared for me so greatly in the months of my illness? Where were my own relatives at this very moment – which could very well have been my last?

'Now I want you to count down from 10,' the orderly said. I began: '10... 9...' As the anaesthesia took effect, I felt every muscle in my body relax, every burden lift. 'Such a wonderful feeling,' I thought. 'I wonder if this is what it's like to die.' And then there was nothing more.

❖

5.1 Complying with the social obligation

'Hey man, bring some water for us!'

I looked over at the man who had called out to me so rudely. It was my younger sister's marriage, and this guy was from the groom's family – a rather domineering man who seemed to have no end of demands for Maa and me. The marriage ceremony had concluded, and we had all graduated upstairs to continue the celebration.

I was in my peak teenage years – hardly a man yet, but with Papa departed and my elder brother nowhere in sight, I knew I had to do what he said. A member of the bride's immediate family is obliged to serve the groom's family. According to our tradition, this man had every right to make such a request – even if the water he wanted was already within arm's length of him just behind him.

I jumped to my feet and went over to him, picked up a few water bottles and held them out to him. 'Water, sir?' I offered. He grabbed one of the bottles and snatched it out of my hand.

'Give me that,' he snarled. 'What kind of place is this that I have to demand water? And look at this place!' He motioned to the ceiling in all directions. Inside I could feel anger beginning to rise just as his voice was rising, but I kept quiet.

'This place is really a dump,' he said, twisting the cap off his bottle. He took a swig, and continued. 'Is this all you think of your sister? I've been to better beer halls.' He chortled, looking at his friends, who joined in with the derisive laughter.

Normally, if someone spoke to me in such a manner they would receive a bang on the face, but in our culture there are conventions for a marriage which we must observe. Accordingly, I bit my tongue, said nothing, turned away and walked downstairs with as much composure as I could muster.

In my mind, I heard Baba's voice echo: 'What does a good man do, Ashu?'

As I made the effort not to stomp my feet on the stairs, I answered him under my breath: 'He restrains himself, Baba.'

In my memory I could hear Baba's hearty laugh, and again his words echoed, 'Yes, yes, Ashu… indeed we do.'

❖

5.2 Compromising with sentiments

'Hey Ashu, when are you going to Aurangabad to join the company?' My brother asked. He was not unaware that for joining a new company, I required some initial money to settle myself in a new town.

'Still trying to arrange some funds. Maybe Fua could help,' I replied in despair.

'Don't worry I will arrange from somewhere if you won't get from Fua,' my brother replied.

My brother tried to help me invariably, but this time he was running very short on money and was already in debt. There were a lot of outstanding payments to settle after my sister's marriage.

'How can you arrange the funds, bhaiya? I know your are already in debt.'

'It's true we are facing a tough time, bhai. But I can't risk your aspirations and dreams just because we are running a financial hardship. We need to find ways to get you through this offer and provide money for that. Having you in a job is among my foremost responsibilities. Moreover, a tag of an engineering graduate will yield lots of money from your dowry to settle all my debt and still more wealth to deposit in the bank for a better future. How can I risk my bright future?' He chuckled.

His laugh could not help me in my despair. My question remained unanswered. How would he manage the money? With this though wheeling in my mind, I couldn't stop myself to pump him for further details.

'But how will the money come, bro?' I asked.

'Well Ashu, I don't have an exact answer to your question at this point in time, but there are options to arrange funds,' Bhaiya said.

I knew Papa left very little for us, which was exhausted in my studies and later in our sister's marriage. My brother was still struggling with the government, to get a compensate job (government provided job to any member of the departed employee's family to meet their financial needs). So what options was he talking about!

'What is it Bhai? What options you are referring to?' I asked.

'We have our father's car. We can sell it to get money for your relocation,' he said.

That would be the last thing I would do. Papa loved his car and in his lifetime he would have never thought of disposing it for freaking money.

'But Bhai, it's papa's favourite car and we value it much more than just a vehicle. It's a token of love from him. I can feel his presence in this car. Every time I sit in this car, I am reminded of Papa. The memories of traveling together as a family come back like a breath of fresh air. Don't you still remember how we used to break into the car to purloin our favourite audio cassette? Don't you still remember how we used to be pigheaded to listen to Papa's advice of not joining him and would jump in the car to accompany him in the last minute every time he would go outstation for some work?'

He was staring at me, his expression turning from a blank to a painful one.

'Bhai, I won't let you sell this car. Please don't do it. We will find some other ways to get the money. I am sure Fua would help.'

'Bhai, I wish we get the money for you very soon. But owning this car now is like owning a white elephant. We don't even have the money to maintain it. It's true when you say we have some emotional connect with this car, but at the same time, we cannot ignore that we also need the money right now. We can buy a car again; it is just a materialistic possession.'

It was hard to believe my ears. How could my brother be so jarring to my senses! But later when I realized my family responsibilities, I found it true that these possessions were just meant to comfort us and should not be associated with sentiments. When they become liabilities, it's better to dispose them.

The company I was joining did not pay during the first month, more like unpaid probation. So those days were a financial hardship for me and my family. Fua had retired from service, so she came up and helped me as much as she could, to arrange funds for food and lodging for that first month.

I was employed with one of the core companies of our branch (electronics and instrumentation) in Aurangabad. We used robotic automation to build various products. It was a typical factory; items moved along a conveyor belt, and at different points along the way a robot would pick each item up, weld a part onto it, then put it back down. The item would move on, and the robot would pick up the next one, and so on. My job was to oversee the robots and program them to handle jobs of different shapes and sizes.

While this may sound fun and interesting, I've left out the most important part – the heat. Welding is a very hot process, and robots give out heat as they function too. So every day was filled with hours and hours in very high temperatures.

My dream was to work for an IT company where there would be none of this heat. I thought that kind of job would be 'cool' in more ways than one! The pay at Aurangabad was relatively low, so practically from day one, I was looking for better opportunities. After a few months I received a letter about an off campus drive for IBM in Noida. I really wanted this job, so I decided to risk everything and just go for it. I quit my job, bought train tickets, and went to.

I called Fua, elated with the news of the interview call. 'Hey Fua! I got an interview call from a very big IT company in Delhi.'

That's good to know, beta. But how would you go to Delhi? You have just joined here and I don't think you would be able to convince them for leave at this time,' she asked.

'You know my dream job was to work in an IT company and I don't think it would be wise not give it a try. I believe I will clear this interview,' I explained.

She believed in me, but I got to know later that my relatives had again got down to criticizing my decision. Despite all odds, I sailed through the interview and my career in IT began. I first started off in the Production domain, working night shifts, then eventually in Development as a programmer.

Initially I stayed as a paying guest in Noida, but soon moved into a flat. My elder brother had gotten married and Fua wanted Maa to come live with me to care for me. She convinced both of us, and we adjusted to the change fairly easily.

I have a memory of my mother spoon-feeding me as a child, but since I mostly lived with Fua in my later years, this was the first time she and I were staying together. I felt lucky to have her with me. Even though I was certain Maa would find things to keep her occupied, it wasn't long before I was concerned that she may be getting bored and lonely at home. Her telephonic conversations with Fua increased around this time and she began talking to me about marriage proposals.

❖

5.3 Head of the household

One day, my phone rang.

'Hello?' I answered, a bit concerned. I wasn't expecting the call. It was one of my brothers-in-law.

'Hey,' he said. 'You need to get here right away. Your brother has been in an accident!'

Inside, I could feel the familiar panic rising. 'Not again,' I thought. 'Please don't let this happen again.'

I choked back tears. 'Is he... is he okay?' I asked.

'Just come... come immediately,' he said sternly. After we ended the call, I tried to reach other relatives, but none of them would answer the phone.

I thought to myself, 'This can't be good.' My concern was growing with their silence; I began to think of the worst scenarios possible. Disha calmed me down and said I must be positive.

I rushed to my room, grabbed my laptop and booked a ticket on the next flight to Patna. We told Maa that we had been called back to our home town immediately, then headed for the airport. Just a few minutes into the ride, my phone rang again; this time it was one of my cousins.

'He's gone,' he said.

Gone. Again. Like Baba and Papa. Just like that, my brother was no more.

Death is a part of life – we all come to understand that at a very young age. But that doesn't make losing a loved one any less painful. And when death comes to a young man so unexpectedly, well... it can really be difficult to accept.

After Papa's death, my brother had become the head of our family. He had cared for Maa, arranged my younger sister's wedding, and helped me through college. I had become used to hearing from him frequently. He always encouraged me in my dreams and aspirations, just as Papa would have. But now he was gone too.

'It can't be,' I thought. 'We were just chatting last night, and he said he was going to visit.' I just couldn't wrap my mind around it.

How is it possible to be making plans one evening, living vibrantly, then the very next morning be gone from this world? The flight seemed to take forever, and we sat in stunned silence most of the way.

We arrived and immediately I saw my brother's body on the veranda, as is our custom. His three-year-old child was next to him, trying to wake him. My bhabhi had told him his papa was sleeping. She was weeping nearby, so we made our way to her.

'How difficult life will be for them without him,' I thought as we tried to comfort her.

I knew grief. I knew how devastating it could be. I had gone through it after Baba left us, and again when Papa was gone.

I could hear a woman moaning loudly from the house. It was Maa. My heart sank. First she had lost her husband, and now her son. If I was finding it difficult to accept my brother's death, how must it be for her? We did our best to comfort her, but she remained inconsolable.

I was the only male member alive in my family now, so the rituals of the sanskar karma had to be accomplished by me. I shouldered his body to the bank of the Ganges for cremation. The priest handed me a burning flame to put it on his body.

'Don't put my father on fire,' the little kid said to me sternly, with anger in his voice.

'Aah, how would I give fire to my brother's body? How could that kid condone setting his own father on fire? Won't this impact his mind. Why was he required to see the rituals of cremation?' I thought.

I was already troubled by the pain and suffering he would be acquainted to on learning what devastation he was witnessing. I couldn't forget the stringent feeling of guilt which ran across me on hearing his words.

I was then hesitant to hold the fire in my hand; his words had hit me hard. In a fit of emotion, I denied to proceed. But it being a social obligation, all the people around persuaded me to perform the ritual and the only answer I got for the kid to be associated with the ritual was - Even being small it was important for him to participate in the ritual as per our tradition.

I would never let this happen had I been the one to decide. But our families value traditional norms so much, that the fear of any change in the traditional way of doing things can cloud their reason.

As the days of the *sanskar karma* went on, I was relieved to see my *bhabhi*'s brothers caring for her. Gradually I came to understand: I was now truly the head of my household. The responsibilities I had carried for Fua and Maa after the deaths of Baba and Papa now fell fully upon me. Knowing that my *bhabhi*'s brothers would take care of their sister would be one comfort during this difficult transition.

Once the rituals had ended, Disha and I took Maa with us, not leaving her behind in such grief. Little did we know how soon things were going to change. But one good did come from all of it. Maa began to turn toward godly devotion for support – a turn that no doubt helped see us through the trials we soon faced.

❖

Crucial substances like vitamins, minerals, and iron are stored in liver cells, to be used by the body as needed.

पीला / *Peela : Yellow : knowledge and learning; success*

Becoming the head of one's household is a solemn event, because it almost always comes because of the loss of a loved one. In our tradition, the men carry this burden heavily, knowing that the eyes of their family are upon them, and that failure is not an option. Although the women in our culture suffer the grief – perhaps to an even deeper level than the men, especially when they are mothers – they are usually able to mourn under the care of others in the family.

For us men, however, the grief of the loss is often shoved aside as we tend to the practical matters of the sanskar karma, the payment for all the services related to the rituals, and the adjustments which must be made within the affected households.

Traditionally in my family, these two roles rarely crossed. The women wept; the men too, as they went about the business of making arrangements. At my brother's death, however, things were different. I was no longer local, so the arrangements had been taken care of before I arrived.

It seems times are changing now, I hope for the better. I can now see equality prevail among men and women, even when burning funeral pyres is concerned. I have known many families who forbid women from entering cremation grounds, leave aside performing cremation rites. But have you ever thought about it? Are these women not the wives, daughters and sisters of those who have passed away? They are also bread winners for many families. They are equal in every sphere of life, if not steps ahead. They merely can't be spectators sitting at home.

Chapter 6

Diagnosis, Travel and Fever

नारंगी / *Narangi : Orange*

I don't have any memories from the time I went to sleep under anesthesia until I awoke in the recovery room. I can only imagine what it was like for Disha as they wheeled me away. If our places were switched, I might have been overwhelmed with thoughts of losing her.

But Disha and I are different people; her mind does not spin over these concerns the way mine does. I expect that as they wheeled me into surgery, her thoughts remained positive, filled with prayers for a successful transplant, followed by a long and healthy life together.

We can never know what the future holds, but our 'present' is made better when we hold on to hope, picturing the best possible outcomes. These pictures turn real if you believe in them. When Disha and I were separated on other occasions, she always went into them telling me that it was only for a short time, and that one day our life together would be secure. It remains our hope that this time is coming soon.

❖

6.1 Celebration

'Hurry, hurry!' Aradhya said, dancing her way down the sidewalk. 'We don't want to miss a minute of Holi!'

'Of course we don't,' her mother chided, 'but Holi isn't going anywhere!'

Disha laughed at our niece's antics and nudged her sister. 'She reminds me of your childhood, Chandani. Her innate qualities and characteristics are very similar to yours,' she said quietly, hoping Aradhya would not hear.

'I'm nothing like Mamma!' the child shrieked, pulling her mouth down in a mocking impression of her mother's face. 'Mamma doesn't know how to have fun! She always stops me from going out to play.'

Disha and her sister laughed loudly at the girl in her silliness, and began recalling for her many stories of their days of fun before the responsibilities of life settled in.

We followed the child down the street cheerfully, our hearts soaring. It was Holi – my favourite festival – and we could already smell the wonderful foods of the downtown Noida celebration from blocks away. I smiled broadly at Aradhya as she took my hands, and together we danced in circles in front of Disha and her sister.

'You should have driven us here,' Disha's sister teased. We had recently gotten a car, but Disha seemed hopeless as a driver. While I had ridden bikes and was easily able to transfer that familiarity with the roads into driving a car, Disha had no such experience to draw upon. Each time I handed her the keys, I prayed her two rounds of driving academy training would kick in, and that she would be able to avoid further dents and scratches to the vehicle. But in reality, it was always me who caused dents and scratches on the car. Disha drove quite cautiously. Slow, but steady.

'Come on, it is Holi!' Disha laughed. 'Don't bring our spirits down by talking about my driving!'

As we neared the celebrating crowds, we picked up some of the coloured water for which the festival is known. Without warning, Chandani turned to me and poured the colourful water on my shoulder, the colour splashing across my face as I yelped in surprise.

'Hey!' I shouted. Turning to her, I aimed for her arm, but Disha stepped in the way. My stream of water landed solidly on her stomach. She laughed out loud and sent a stream of her own colour back onto my chest, then quickly had to look away as Aradhya's stream of colour sailed just past her face.

'I almost got you!' Aradhya screamed, turning her colour water stream to me next. She and I exchanged streams, both of us now glowing with multiple colours as we entered the crowd.

Holi has always been my favourite festival. I love the colours and the cuisine, especially *malpua*, a sweet dish similar to pancakes (but without the syrup). Most of the foods prepared for Holi are not enjoyed any other time. This makes them particularly special, as we look forward to them each year.

I remember this particular Holi vividly, especially Aradhya. She is a very classy, grown-up kid from Delhi – but so cute! We have watched her grow into the impressive six-year-old she is now.

But if you ask her, she can't grow up fast enough – every year she asks over and over, 'How many months until my birthday?'

Aradhya refuses to call Disha *mausi*; she insists on calling us both by name. I love how she talks, and especially how excited she gets over each new thing. We could all learn something from children in this regard. As adults, we sometimes have to muster up motivation to tackle the day, but children have a natural motivation and excitement, looking at every new day as a new opportunity. Not only that, but they rejoice over a new toy or doll, and giving them a bigger one would not make their joy any greater – they know how to celebrate what they have to the full.

❖

6.2 Joyful days

'Hey Ashu, let's go for a ride!' Disha tried coaxing me for a ride, while I was still fast asleep.

'Let me sleep some more, Disha. We can go later in the noon, it's very early,' I said.

She always managed to cajole me into doing what she wanted. I had to agree to her every time, without fail. so this time too, I woke up reluctantly.

'Where are we going?' I asked yawning.

Seeing my unwillingness and lack of enthusiasm, she refrained from a reply and pulled the car keys from the holder. She rushed out of the house to the parking lot. I followed her. I could feel she was getting angry. I had promised her a few days back that we would go driving early morning as it would be easy for her to practice in lesser traffic.

Long before I could run to the parking, she raced the car through the driveway to the entrance gate of the society and was waiting for me to get in. Her wrath could be felt in her silence. Without another word, she drove the car like a rocket. I felt I should warn her about the high speed while taking steep turns along the course, but preferred not to speak. It would have poked her further, raising her anguish, eventually ending up with a still higher speed. I chose to be silent and beheld her wrath. She looked amazing even when she was angry.

Early morning rides are actually fun, because there is very little traffic. Once the traffic sets in during the peak timings, driving becomes exasperating.

In a few minutes, I realized we were moving towards Noida. Daily commute for office had made me familiar to the route. There was only one place where we could be going, but why was she going to her sister's place so early? My mind was thumping to find an answer as we raced to Noida.

I sighed in relief on reaching, sure that we were now safe. Disha stepped out of the car and smashed the door. She anyway never closed the door gently, and her anger was the icing on the cake.

On reaching their home, I made myself comfortable on the sofa and started playing with Aradhya. She ws overwhelmed with enthusiasm on our visit, like always. 'It's Mama's birthday,' she whispered in my ears. In seconds, I could correlate why we were there.

Few minutes of gossips with her sister would let Disha forget everything and she would come to me with love, I presumed. But this was not to happen. At least she started a conversation, made me feel relieved. I would apologize to her later, I thought.

She asked me to go out and bring a cake and some samosas for everyone.

'I love samosas,' Aradhya yelled in happiness.

'Even I love hot and crispy samosas,' I replied fascinatingly.

I wasn't sure where I could get all that so early in the morning, but I cranked the engine of my car and went in quest for samosas and cake. After about an hour of exploring , I found a shop opened. I already knew about the shop and had some positive feedback of its quality. So I got samosas packed for everyone, and also bought a cake from a nearby shop.

I drove back to Aradhya's place hurriedly as I didn't want the samosas to turn cold and soggy. I also brought some chicken rolls as I knew Disha loved them. I was sure she would forget everything in its wonderful taste and my apologies would be granted easily.

These were days of freedom and joy for all of us. Disha and I had moved to a large flat, and she had done a wonderful job of decorating the place. With the increased income from my IT job and Disha's promotion, we had purchased the car.

By god's grace, our relationship was going well too. We would ride together to work, which during the rainy season was rather time-consuming. I used to get irritated – especially when the time sitting in traffic cut into the work day and resulted in less pay for me – but Disha always encouraged me to look at the brighter side, to enjoy the weather and the rain.

But we had days when she would need some pepping up from me. I can recall times when she and I would have a difference of opinion, and sometimes we would even fight as we drove to work. When this would happen, I would go down to the thelas and pick up some chicken dimsum or a chicken roll for her. She would always give me a look of exasperation, because she knew what I was doing. But no matter how hard she tried to refuse my gift, I would insist she take it. Once it was open, the wonderful aroma would soften her heart and she would begin to enjoy the delectable treat, sometimes even sharing it with me. Before long, we would forget our differences, revelling in the wonderful smells and flavour of the food.

I was never one to stay at home, and I can remember during this time we would often use the car to go to places like Agra, Mathura, Mussoorie or Haridwar – all places near Delhi, ideal for weekend trips. We would also go to the movies, sometimes on our own and other times with Aradhya and Chandani. Many such plans were made at the spur of the moment – we would just decide to go, jump in the car, and pick a movie. Being foodies, we always stocked up on the concessions: chicken nuggets, sweet corn, popcorn and cold drinks.

We also made good use of the car by driving Aradhya and Chandani taking Aradhya to day care and dropping Chandani off at work before we went to our own jobs. Chandani and her husband are bank officials with very busy schedules, and Disha and I were happy for the extra time with our entertaining niece. When she got off work, Disha would pick Aradhya up before me, and we would enjoy driving around until Chandani's work day ended and we took them home. It became a routine we all enjoyed, particularly as Aradhya became more inquisitive and observant. Sometimes she would amaze us when a song came on the radio – she could almost always identify the artist or the movie the song was from before the rest of us could!

These were good times; they are a bright spot on the horizon of my life when I look at it as a whole. Good times, yes, but all too brief.

❖

6.3 The diagnosis

The flickering of the strobe lights whipped across my feeble body as I staggered back from the crowd dancing on beats reverbating through the loudspeakers and woofers of the club.

I practically bent over at my waist as the sting from the pain made me groan. It was getting intense with every chord stuck by the DJ. I kept wiping my face. My eyes kept darting around. And I didn't know exactly what was happening. I had to get out of here. This was way too much for me to take in.

My eyes scanned the crowd, searching for Disha. I caught a glimpse of Shrawan jumping up and down to the music, screaming at the top of his lungs and completely oblivious to the fact that I was missing. My back fell against the brick wall of the club. I held Disha's shoulders as she popped up from somewhere. My vision was getting blurred and the beats getting vauge as I sank on my knees.

Disha crouched leaning forward. She cupped my cheeks to ask if I was alright. I was gasping heavily, sweat oozing out from my forehead like rain. Disha was dumbstruck, but gathered herself and ran into the crowd to find Shrawan.

She grabbed his arm. 'Shrawan!'

He looked at her. 'What?'

'We have to leave. Now!' He furrowed his brow but didn't question. All he did was nod his head before his own eyes started darting around. I knew he was looking for me. Disha pulled him out of the crowd and over to the side where I already had poised towards the exit.

'What's going on? What's wrong?' he asked.

'Just stay quiet and follow me! Ashu is struggling to catch his breath, he is sweating heavily. We need to rush to the hospital,' Disha explained.

Shrawan rushed to me, asking with concern, 'Are you alright?' he asked.

'Can't you see he is stumbling. Help me shoulder him out from this freaking club,' Disha screamed.

They both hustled me out through a hallway that dumped into an alley.

'Hold him, Shrawan,' Disha said as she ran to pull the car out of the parking lot.

They both held my arms and helped me get into the car. While Disha sat beside me, Shrawan cranked the engine to gear up for the drive.

My lower lip quivered. I felt my entire body shaking. My shoulder collasped, and my entire body wrinkled. It felt like my body was trying to cave it on itself. Disha slid her hands over my shoulder and rubbed and massaged my back muscles to relieve some of the panic. Tears rushed from her eyes, and the best she could do was to express guilt on going to the club. I think I also had very high temperature, because every time Disha touched my forehead, she screamed at Shrawan to accelerate.

Nurses wheeled me to a waiting desk before they would let me in. A form had to be filled by Disha. Seeing me groaning, Shrawan ran past us as he blazed a trail down the hallway, slamming through the doors and following to the sign of the emergency room. Disha jogged behind him as the attendant wheeled me towards her.

He took a grinding halt when he found a doctor sitting.

'Sir, please admit him first, we can do the formalities later,' he howled.

Disha too pleaded with him to admit me urgently with admission formalities to follow.

'Sister, please let him in and lay him down on the gurney. We can do the formalities once all his vitals are monitored.'

A little while later, I woke up normal. Blood samples had been sent to the lab and we were waiting for the reports to come. I was taken aback when blood tests revealed a high level of bilirubin and an alarmingly low platelet count (almost 30,000 where the normal range is over 150,000). An ultrasound was performed which revealed decompensated chronic liver disease.

It is hard to put into words how this news affected me. I knew, based on the experience with my father, that this was an incurable condition. I knew that because of the disease, my liver would continue to deteriorate and would eventually fail. Doctors did not have to tell me, because I already knew: without a transplant, my condition could only get worse.

I was diagnosed with advanced liver disease in the middle stages of the condition. Some may wonder how I could be so ill and not already know it. This is not uncommon with liver disease. Even acute cases may not show symptoms till the liver has suffered 70% damage. In the initial stages, blood tests are close to normal and the mild symptoms like itching and skin irritation can be dismissed as having other causes.

It seemed like I had just begun to build such a beautiful life with Disha and our families. And now, suddenly, all of that crashed down around me. The news hit Disha hard too. I could see her shock, and she seemed to be worried for the first time. Seeing my beautiful, optimistic wife having such concern haunted me. I felt guilty over it. I started hating myself for spoiling our wonderful life together.

My relatives did not help matters. Many of them began to speculate that, like my father, I had brought the disease on myself by excessive drinking. Somehow the first reaction of anyone in such cases is related to alcohol consumption. In my feelings of shame, there was a time when I even wondered about this myself – I knew I had been a beer lover in college. But it takes at least a decade of alcohol abuse to have such an effect on the liver. I had been drinking a much shorter time than that. Disha forbade my relatives from sharing their speculations with me, but I found out later that my poor mother became victim to their jeering. Instead of worrying for my health, those relatives worried only over what had caused the disease and how much money would be involved in its treatment.

❖

6.4 Travel

Health-wise, I had bounced back somewhat. My primary doctor, Dr Vibhu, met me regularly and corresponded often via phone, email and messaging. Along with the other doctors at the hospital, he had estimated that it could be three to five years before my liver disease became debilitating. I had strictly followed Dr Vibhu's advice, and by adjusting my diet, I was able to live a relatively normal life in those early days.

In an effort to pull me out of my increasing depression, Disha suggested we get the doctors to approve some travel, hoping that a change of scenery would help lift my mood.

Thailand seemed a good first destination; it was affordable and intriguing. So Disha worked with travel planners to make all the arrangements, barely letting me in on the plans at all.

"This trip is exactly what we need," Disha said as she loaded our luggage into the taxi. "A few days in Thailand will let us forget all of this sadness. Let's go see something new!"

Reluctantly, I helped her with the largest bag. Since my diagnosis, nothing seemed to bring me joy.

"Dishu, I always thought of making a very beautiful life with you, but I failed. And instead of the wonderful life you deserved, all I could offer you now is illness and dying," I whimpered.

"Nonsense!" she said. "We will not let this ruin our lives. We are going to Thailand, and we are going to love it!"

When we landed in Bangkok after almost five hours of starting from home, I felt tired to the bones. We rested that day and decided to stay in. We had planned things from the next day onward, and Disha was really excited about it.

Vexatious chimes of the call bell spared no chance for me to carry through the wonderful moment with Disha the next morning. I was leaning on her shoulders, talking love when a lady knocked on the door, screaming in the hallway. "Hurry up! You guys are never on time."

We hustled to her screams without bothering much. We were ready anyway, and went out to board the traveler assigned to us for the day.

In due course, the car made its way through beautiful scriptures and paintings flanked all along a building. I was smitten by the sheer beauty and wondered if it was a Buddhist temple. Scrolling down the itinerary on my phone, I wondered if any such visit was part of the specified plans.

“Hello everyone, this is one of the oldest temples in town. We will start our expedition from this serene place. We can cover all the other destinations as mentioned in your itinerary later.”

We all stepped out of the bus. The weather was very pleasant, yet Disha hadn’t missed to bring the neck gaiter for me. She feared the blowing winds may knock me down. I never wore them, but she kept it handy.

We both travelled the expanse of the fascinating Wat Pho temple. Few photos with the magnificent statue of lord Buddha in the temple were sufficient, and I was heading out when I spotted some monks eating something inside the premises of the temple.

‘Holy shit, is he gnawing at non-veg in the temple?’

‘Yes, Buddhism lets you eat anything, once it’s on your plate. You are free to eat anywhere and anything, given that you don’t inflict violence on the animals you are eating,’ Disha explained.

That is so very interesting. I find this to be very different from our culture in India, where food restrictions are observed based on days and places and people always seem to be trying to find a flaw in the taste of everything they eat. (I have to say, I like the Buddhist approach to food!).

‘The fun will unwrap itself with every adventure ride in Pattaya now. We’ll love it, Dishu.” I said with a smile, scrolling down the itinerary on my phone.

“I am glad you are liking it,” she replied.

The sea beach in Pattaya was much like the beaches I had seen in India; the only difference I noticed was the color of the water. The sea around Thailand is blue, whereas in India it is white. The beaches themselves are very clean, with easy chairs to help people relax. There is no restriction regarding alcohol, which means you can drink anything you like as you bathe in the sun. We sat for hours on the beach, talking and gossiping. Disha kept me laughing and happy. I believe this is a big part of why I was able to live so normally, even while suffering an acute liver disease.

Next morning, we were all set for the coral island. This had to be a great experience, I was sure. The island was half an hour away from the beach, with one station in between with scads of adventure activities all around.

'Shall we try any of these, Disha? I mean, there are plenty of them to choose from. I can try scuba diving; it seems relatively less exhausting, yet much fun.' I tried to persuade Disha.

'No Ashu. Once you are better, we will have a word tour, I promise. You do whatever you want to then.'

'You are saying this as if you are sure I will be good in the future. What if I fade even more? Anyway, let's not spoil the mood," I said in an uncomprehending way.

There had been many situation when I didn't see eye to eye with Disha's future-seeking attitude. Traitorous rebellion thrived in me whenever she stopped me from doing something and postponed it to the future. But now, with recovery, all my held-back aspirations of fascinating adventures are being fulfilled.

Thailand was like a breath of fresh air for me. We felt free to enjoy ourselves, and we visited sites like the undersea aquarium and even saw an elephant show. The elephants were impressive and fun. I was amazed how they were trained to play football and paint. Also, although we did not try it, the street food there is quite famous. They have economical continental cuisine, including Indian as well as Arabic, and a lot of sea food, chicken, fruit and vegetables.

If there is one area we found challenging to adjust to, it was a lower standard of service. In India, we are used to receiving high quality services from establishments where the staff is very professional, polite and respectful. In Thailand, the people in the service industry can be more difficult. We found them to be getting impatient, or getting irritated with the demands of the customers. Thankfully, we were accompanied by people assigned by the travel agency, and they made sure we had everything we needed.

The travel did me good, and every weekend after we returned home from Thailand, I would scope out a place for us to visit. Disha rarely denied my requests of travel, only refusing when she had an official trip to take. She was called to the new facility in Pune about twice a month. I went with her a few times and enjoyed the luxury hotel stays provided by her company. It also helped us spend some quality time together.

Making travel, rest and relaxation a priority kept my stress levels lowered, and this helped me withstand the various tests, visits to doctors and hospitalizations that accompany liver disease. I was hospitalized on three separate occasions prior to my transplant. So visiting these different locations gave me an opportunity to reset my body and mind, and allowed me to interact with people of different cultures, which improved my social skills too.

Looking back, I feel so much gratitude that I am blessed with a wife who was able to make these times possible for me. Disha held a position with her company which brought in sufficient income that we never had to worry over the expense of these small trips. Instead of sitting at home worrying over my condition, we were able to enjoy a bit of extravagance and take our minds off these things.

❖

6.5 Travel and fever

At one point, I began to have frequent fever that the doctors could not explain, other than to state the obvious point: it was related to my liver disease.

Disha texted Dr Vibhu about my condition, and he advised admitting me in a hospital for a few days, for observation.

I have to admit that I had feared going into the hospital. Those places always seemed to me to be full of sick and dying people, so I expected it to be very unpleasant. But it was not so dreadful with Disha and Shrawan by my side.

The very next day of my hospital admission, Shrawan walked into my hospital room, elated.

'Hey buddy, guess what! My engagement date has been announced.'

The overwhelming happiness of him getting engaged put forth all other emotions that entangled us. He couldn't resist from sharing his joy with Disha. We made even a hospital room so much amicable and pleasant that mere thought of illness and disease stepped down from my mind. Even in the unfavourable state and adversities, we enjoyed the little bits of happiness.

Before much longer, Disha was given the opportunity to go on an official trip to Singapore. We decided that it was within our budget for me to join her, so together we stayed in the company guest house. It had all of the amenities of a luxury hotel, so I very much enjoyed the stay. Thanks to the "work from home" arrangement with FSG, I was even able to work as we travelled.

We set off to explore Singapore on the weekends. Pleasant weather aided and abetted me to run into the expanses of a small but profoundly interesting country. The beauty of the flower dome beckoned us while traversing into the surreal sights of lush and green gardens.

Soothing breeze thriving from the adjacent Marina Bay waterfront whipped through the leaves before touching my face. I lay down on Disha's lap for hours, girdling her hairs around my fingers in this serene environment.

Seeing a distant cruise ship berthed on a platform in the waterfront, I asked her.

'Are we going for a cruise? Since my childhood, every time I saw a ship or an advertisement for a cruise, waves of exhilaration swept over me.' I pleaded to Disha.

'I don't think it will be wise to travel far from land without much medical assistance. I assure we will travel sometime in future.'

'But Dishu, you know I find the idea of going on a cruise mesmerizing. Spending days on the dark blue sea, far from land, with nights under a star-studded sky… nothing around but the majestic sea and the unfathomable depths below. It's a dream I hold from my childhood.'

In spite of these setbacks, Disha and I remained determined to enjoy our lives, and for us that meant travel. Prior to my hospitalizations, Disha's brother Shrawan had gotten engaged, so we had planned a visit to our hometown. After my discharge, Disha expressed concern that perhaps I should stay in Delhi, but I spoke to the doctor just prior to our planned travel dates and got approval for the trip. A party was planned, but on a smaller scale, that included only close relatives (so that I would not be overly taxed by the social gathering). Our family went out of their way to accommodate my condition, even preparing food especially to meet my dietary restrictions. I thoroughly enjoyed celebrating with them; we were all very happy to be able to be together.

In spite of these setbacks, Disha and I remained determined to enjoy our lives, and for us that meant travel. Prior to my hospitalizations, Disha's brother Shrawan had gotten engaged, so we had planned a visit to our hometown. After my discharge, Disha expressed concern that perhaps I should stay in Delhi, but I spoke to the doctor just prior to our travel dates and got approval for the trip. A party was planned, but on a smaller scale, that included only close relatives (so that I would not be overly taxed by the social gathering). Our family went out of their way to accommodate my condition, even preparing food especially to meet my dietary restrictions. I thoroughly enjoyed celebrating with them; we were all very happy to be together.

❖

That same year, I came down with a heavy cough and cold which got worse and worse until finally they admitted me into the ICU with extremely low oxygen levels. Unlike the prior hospital stay, where I had been discharged after a couple of days, this one was a very bitter experience: I had a breathing tube through my nose and was unable to sleep due to a machine next to my bed that beeped throughout the night. All night I lay there, miserable and wishing I was back home.

I don't know what it is about an ICU – it seems like something torments you there. After the longest night of my life, I convinced a doctor to move me to 'step down ICU', where I had a bit more freedom (just that I could answer nature's call on my own). I stayed there six more hours until another doctors' team came to check my vitals. Although they never identified a specific cause for my oxygen saturation to have dropped so low, they finally moved me to a regular room where the levels gradually improved. After a few more days, they were back to normal and I was discharged. Later, nearer the time for my transplant, further tests showed that I suffered hepatopulmonary syndrome (HPS), a condition common in patients with liver disease.

❖

Bile is essential to the body: without it, fats are not digested and toxins build up. Making bile is a key function of the liver.

नारंगी / *Narangi : Orange*

When someone receives a diagnosis like chronic liver disease, it's very easy to slide into hopelessness and worry. Thanks to Disha and her ability to rise above all of that and introduce me to the joys of travel, the diagnosis which could have meant the end of me became the cause of a changed life. Instead of dwelling on my circumstances as I had a tendency to do, we made an adventure of it.

If you know someone who is facing terminal illness or a devastating disease, I encourage you to help them escape the prison of themselves… to try a change of scenery and meet people of different lands. While it may not cure them or even reduce their suffering, it will give them a sense of living that they otherwise may not ever experience, and give them a chance to dream of better times and better places… to plan for a day when their current restrictions are gone, and they can once again live a full life.

Chapter 7

Disha's Departure

नीला / *Neela : Blue : bravery and stability; insight, thought*

Chronic liver disease has no cure – those who suffer from it may make adjustments in diet and lifestyle to slow the progression toward liver failure, but the only hope for recovery is a transplant. This seems easy, but reality is very different. One needs to seek a prospective live donor within close relationship. If that works out, you have some reason to celebrate, else you have to rely on the cadaveric donor (DDLT method). This is where the hassles of marathon surgery starts. The list of patients requiring new livers is very long, with thousands of them waiting for years, so the chances of receiving a donor is very sleek.

India is one of the countries that offers the option of cadaveric transplantation – this means the liver for transplant comes from a patient who has been pronounced 'brain-dead,' without life-sustaining brain activity, and with no hope for recovery. (Organs cannot be taken from patients who have completely died; the blood in them clots too quickly.)

But receiving an organ is still not a guarantee of recovery. There are risks involved with the surgery itself. The recipient's body may reject the organ, the potential for infection after a transplant is high, and there can be other complications.

When I received my new liver, it truly seemed miraculous. People can wait for a liver transplant for years, but mine became available to me within three months after my condition began rapidly deteriorating. From the day I was diagnosed, the odds seemed stacked against me, yet here I am today – healthy and recovering steadily. I credit Disha's faith, and her encouragement to keep me thinking positively to overcome the odds. Also, the need for funds pulled our families together in sacrifice. God has indeed smiled on us.

❖

7.1 New house

When Disha and I returned from Singapore, life quieted down a bit. We were doing well financially, and we decided it would be good to relocate to a better location. We applied for a home loan and soon found a wonderful flat with a spacious floor plan and balconies. When Disha saw the balcony, she fell in love with it, imagining glorious evenings together, watching the sun set. We were able to open the windows on three sides for fresh air and ventilation, which we knew would be beneficial for my health.

Disha surprised me by diving into the decoration of our new home with enthusiasm. Donning the hat of an interior decorator, she drew up floor plans and a very professional looking presentation to outline, room by room, all the details of her design. To ensure the outcome she expected, her design included every detail, from the paint colours and floor covering down to each piece of furniture – even the TV stand!

As workers progressed toward bringing her design to life over the course of the next three months, Disha and I would stop by almost daily, excited each time to see what had been accomplished since our last visit. In due time, we scheduled the *griha prawesh puja* with our pandit (priest), keeping the event quiet and reserved, as is Disha's way. (She has often reminded me that it is better not to be too showy in such things, as making them widely known – through social media and such other things – is a sure way to bring in some negativity, which she always prohibited from creeping into my life. With the blessings of lord Shiva, we soon moved into our new home. Location-wise, it was nearer to our workplaces, which saved us both time and fuel. It was also next to a park, so we thoroughly enjoyed long walks in the evenings. As the year went on, we made several visits to our hometown too, for the engagements and weddings of our loved ones.

Several months after we moved, Disha received approval for a work visa to the United States. Working in America had been a life-long dream for her. She had made many official visits there, and admired the atmosphere of opportunity there. We began making preparation for relocation, but for me, it seemed unwise. I had a professional obligation which really needed my attention for two more months, and my doctor advised me that my chances of a successful transplant would be diminished if I left the country. Generally speaking, cadaveric transplantation is only done in one's country of origin; few countries make exceptions to this rule. It was a difficult decision for us to part, but knowing that we could use the additional funds toward the expense of a transplant, Disha decided to accept the new opportunity while I remained in India.

In a week's time, her ticket to Denver was booked. I was overwhelmed with emotions. I knew letting her go would choke me in loneliness, but at the same time, I was very happy seeing her achieve success in life and chasing her dreams. How could I stop her from living her dream! I always wished for Disha to excel in her profession and fulfil all her aspiration.

I knew how hard it could be for Disha to adjust in a new environment without me. I knew she always struggled in the cold of Delhi, and to bear the snowing in US, she would need warm clothes and jackets. I took time off from my work to shop for her. Disha didn't let me go anywhere unattended, so as to avoid any chances of infection, but I decided to surprise her and bought some clothes for her. She liked my choice and wore them fondly.

❖

7.2 A travel to divinity

Few days to her departure, we thought of spending some good time together. Disha is very spiritual, but I was usually sceptical about any eternal power carving something divine for me out of the odds. Although I believed in a creator, but not in any magic. I always presumed the priests and the pandits to be penny-pinchers. They would merely make you squander your money in pooja and mantras which they sought as the only solution to your devastation and suffering. With the life threatening disease I carried, it would be a lot easier for them to trick my wife and mother for money. They would simulate some ritual in the name of god and would victimize them for money with their god-fearing mockeries.

I knew Disha is a girl of formidable intelligence and tenacity and she firmly believed that I will be well soon. But I didn't want her to be trapped in such orthodoxy. But Disha coaxed me to visit a serene place in Rajasthan, Mount Abu – the 'Brahma Kumaris Ashram'. The ashram is spread in many acres and is nestled in the valley of the mountain. When I reached the ashram, I was astonished by the tranquillity of the place. It felt like I was away from the all chaos of life. I could feel my mind getting light already. Disha further revealed that the visit didn't require any money paid as charges; it was up to the visitors to pay whatever they felt like. The Ashram administration never made money a compulsion. I quite liked the approach; it was very different from the traditional ashrams I had known.

I was seeking an answer to the question that haunted me – why me? Why was I suffering such a fatal disease? But that was only till I remained alien to the sovereignty of positive thoughts and the teaching of unfolded mystery of life by Brahma Kumaris.

The reply I got was ironic – have you ever asked god why you were rewarded with uncountable blessings?

No, we never do that. It is only when we find things going a bit differently than our expectations, we make god accountable for the plight. But they said ups and downs or rather distress and pleasure are both relative. We must also acknowledge the blessings if we curse the desolation.

I found this true. I don't know about the others, but at least I was blaming god for my misery, never bothering to thank him for the beautiful blessings.

A question still arose in my mind. How does fate decide the quota of happiness or sorrow for every person? I mean, why was I diagnosed with a disease, while others weren't? Even in the world, we find people endowed with prosperity, and some deprived of it. The answer I got was beyond the worldly affairs. Something more spiritual. My mind occluded to accept it or perhaps I was too young to think beyond the materialistic world. I could only apprehend to an extent that it was similar to the moral tale I had heard umpteen times by my grandparents, in which they proclaimed fate of every individual is pronounced by karma. They never bothered to delve deeper into it, or perhaps all they knew was very little.

The unbridled enlightenment of spirituality of the Dadis of the Brahma Kumaris helped me perceive the intended meaning of the word 'karmic account'. I experimented with the power of positive thoughts which is evident in my recovery. They call it '*sankalp se srishti – thoughts create destiny*'. The secret is to start believing in what you want from your life. Inert power will awaken inside you. You will begin to unlock the true potential of your mind to create the kind of magical life that you have envisaged. It is not all plain-sailing to live your thoughts; it really requires a lot of practice. You must not let any negativity to override your belief. In order to get things right, not even a single thought of negativity thriving in your mind could be spared. You need to be firm and unwavering with your faith, only then you can expect the magic of faith and positivity in fruition.

Most of us would be aware of the story of Solomon Islands, where the islanders assembled around a tree and started cursing and yelling at a tree. The negative powers somehow damaged the tree and it fell. This is a mere example of what I am talking about.

We cannot abandon from striving hard to achieve our goals (what we believe will happen) and replace it just by contemplating for a positive outcome. Certainly this is not the way.

Our efforts in unison with our beliefs will work wonders. Only if we believe in achieving our goals, we will work for it with diligence. It would be then that every object of the universe will start shedding energy for us and will conspire with us to work magic in our life.

❖

7.3 Her departure

The day of her departure was an emotional one for me. Many times I had given her a 'send off' on official trips, but this time, things were different. We would be parted for a long time, and I did not know what my illness would bring. I wanted her with me, but I could not ask her to decline this opportunity, and I felt I had to stay back. Disha, as usual, approached our separation with grace, reminding me we could have our 'happily ever after' once my surgery was done. We said our emotional goodbyes, she boarded the plane, and I watched her fly over the horizon.

The months after Disha left were sad ones for me. Not much was changed, everyone was still around me, but her absence left me empty and feeling deserted. Slowly, as the days went by, I got used to the feeling of missing her. She did what she could to make things better, engaging in video calls with me regularly and doing her best to encourage me.

When we spoke, Disha reminded me that our sacrifices were being rewarded; the extra income from her work was necessary for my surgery. She, too, was living alone, and she was walking to work to save as much money as possible. The adjustment was not easy for her either; she was working in Colorado, an unknown place, among people she did not know. She told me she thought of me most when she ate at restaurants there, wishing we could share the experience, as we had with so many meals. But overall, as with everything else, Disha managed the changes well.

For my part, I missed Disha most on the days I had doctor's visits. She had always driven me for the visits, as I was told I should not drive. Since one symptom of advanced liver disease is frequent confusion and drowsiness, driving becomes very risky. My mother was living with me by this time, but she did not drive a car. Thankfully, Disha's brother Shrawan lived nearby, so I knew if I ever needed immediate help, we could contact him.

❖

7.4 Health worsened

I was getting annoyed with my phone buzzing in my ears continuously. It was just an arm's length away on the computer table next to my bed. I knew it could be Disha, calling to share some stories of her presentation and how everyone in her office was impressed with her idea. I didn't want to let her know how sick I was and preferred not to answer. But my phone rang continuously, and reluctantly, I shoved my blanket aside and stepped out of the bed to stretch out again on the sofa. Now at least I could give her an excuse of not picking up the phone for so long. She knew I had a deep sleep and watching TV for long hours was sufficient to send me to a zizz.

I picked her call. I could see how excited she was, waiting to share something enthralling with me. She had an imposing business idea and wanted me to join her. But my mind was tangled in some other thoughts, the everlasting thoughts of getting through the transplant and arranging funds for that. By this time, I already learned that no one from our immediate family could donate a part of their liver to me and the only option left was a dead donor liver transplant, which was thrice the cost of live donor transplant.

A cab driver taunted me over my bloated stomach one day. Even in the office, I could find people making fun of my fluffy stomach. They presumed it was just overeating, overlooking the other reasons of the problem. My face was still the same; it never swelled and was rather shrinking day by day. Although it was very rare that I went to my work place and preferred work from home ever since Disha had left for the US, I had to suffer some humiliation every time I went out.

How could I even pay heed to the words of Disha with these thoughts wheeling in my mind? I tried to offend my thoughts and showed Disha I was listening, by inquiring on some things she was talking about. Disha could not notice my fluffy stomach as she could only see my face on calls. I hid it from her. She somehow sensed my pain and hung up the call, telling me to take care.

In a little while, I heard a knock on the door. 'Ashu, please open the door!' Shrawan was screaming at the door.

Oh, he looked worried. I wondered if Disha had asked him to check on me.

I stood grudgingly and opened the door. Shrawan came in and touched my forehead to check if I had fever.

'My god, you have a soaring temperature. Let me check it. Where is the thermometer?' he asked, a bit scared.

The temperature measured 104 degree. Without further delay, Shrawan took me to the hospital. He showed his discontent on our way to the hospital as to why I hadn't informed him if I was not feeling well.

My mother had been away for the last few days due to some other family priorities and I was alone in the house. I didn't want to make a mess of his newly-married life by calling him so frequently. Having fever was normal for me and the doctor had already prescribed drugs for that. I could have those in a state of high fever, but this time, the medicines were not working.

Shrawan asked me if I had taken the medicine for fever and advised me to rest on the back seat of the car while he was driving. I was groaning in pain every time the car hit the bump.

On reaching hospital the doctor asked me to get an ultrasound to see if ascites(water retention) was severe, I was already diagnosed with mild ascites some days back, when report came Dr Vibhu made me clear that my condition was getting worsened and I needed a transplant at the earliest.

On asking how much time it could be restrained by medicine, he replied it could be even a day for a liver failure. What was he saying? He was contradicting his own words. He had said two years back, 'It could be 3 to 5 years before my transplant'. He ended up telling it's very tough to predict number of days in case of liver disease, so better get the transplant done before it actually fails. Dr Vibhu also said that chances of cadaveric transplants are very less; it's a type of lottery and you could get an organ only if you are lucky.

This conversation was enough to startle me. Shrawan too was scared with what the doctor said and couldn't wait to call Disha to explain the situation. We stayed in the car while Shrawan was conversing with Disha to find ways of transferring me to Chennai.

The dirutics helped me gain my health and in a few days I found myself normal. The visit to Dr Vibhu made it very clear that surgery was imminent and I required it at the earliest.

As time passed and my condition began to worsen, Disha instructed Shrawan to begin taking care of my medicines, doctor's visits and regular blood tests. This worked for a few months, but before long I began having frequent fevers – my temperature soaring every two to three days, accompanied by severe digestive issues. Doctors at Max Hospital in Delhi were unable to determine exactly what was causing these issues. These symptoms continued and progressed; soon I began retaining fluids and the doctors began reminding us about our need for a transplant which was becoming imminent.

After substantial research, we determined it would be best if I relocated to Chennai. There, the chances of receiving a cadaveric liver transplant were higher as compared to other parts of the country. Despite their already substantial debt, family members in both Disha's and my family pooled their resources. My mother withdrew her savings and my elder sister and bhabhi contributed what they could too. I was surprised by this generosity; these were not people who had been close to me all my life. I never would have expected such willingness to help, but together our families made it possible for me to go to Chennai in preparation for surgery.

At this point, I need to tell you about Pradip bhaiya. He is one of Disha's brothers, but to me he is more than just an 'in-law'. I consider him a true brother. I actually cannot put into words how much this man means to me. He is the most responsible, caring, organized person I've ever known. At a very young age, he assumed responsibility for his family and every decision I have seen him make has been prudent and well-thought-out. I will never be able to thank him enough for his help and support throughout my illness – not just the financial support, but also the care with which he made arrangements for Disha and me.

It was Pradip bhaiya who helped Disha decide when it was best to move me to Chennai. He and Shrawan made arrangements to accompany me, and upon our arrival I went to the hospital for a pre-transplant work-up of tests. Immediately the hospital staff in Chennai put me at ease; they were polite and generous, giving me a sense of confidence that they would take care of me during my treatment.

❖

7.5 Pre-transplant evaluation

The pre-transplant tests took four days and included more extensive blood work than I had previously done. Based on these tests, the doctors were able to determine that I had a rare condition called Budd Chiary Syndrome (one in a million) where a blood clot had formed in the hepatic veins. I was also diagnosed with Hepatopulmonary Syndrome, a condition common to patients with liver disease where blood vessels in the lungs broaden. This 'vasodilation' causes shortness of breath and hypoxemia (low oxygen levels). Finally the mystery of my prior ICU visit was solved and I soon realized that it was unlikely that alcohol had contributed to my disease; all along it was blood clots causing the problem!

There was no room for celebration over that, however, as the tests determined, I had advanced liver disease with no time to waste before a transplant. Since we had not been able to identify a live donor, the doctors signed me up the same day on the Tamil Nadu Network for Organ Sharing (TNOS) web portal. A transplant coordinator was assigned who recommended we remain in Chennai. We were told that if cadaveric transplant was to become possible, there would only be six hours from the time the organ became available until the surgery had to be completed.

Pradip bhaiya had seen to it that we stayed in a quality hotel during the tests, but now we had to find lodging suitable for our wait. We needed something near the hospital, dust free, and requiring little interaction with people – all to minimize any risk of post-transplant infections. Shrawan found a good flat for us very close to the hospital – it was newly constructed and very clean. Before long we were settled in, and I was even able to continue working, thanks to FSG's work from home policy. As everything fell into place so quickly and so well for us, my gratitude for everyone's help grew, as did my hope in divine providence.

Shrawan could not stay in Chennai, but Pradip bhaiya was able to make some compromises with his family members and rearrange his professional priorities to stay with me. Maa joined us, and though Chennai never felt like 'home', we had a comfortable stay living there.

Weeks passed, and we visited the hospital regularly to get an update from the surgery coordinator. Initially we were told the surgery should take place within a month, so we scrambled to get the funds deposited in the hospital. The month came and went, and although my blood reports had improved with the regular care, it was difficult to remain patient with the process. Each time we consulted with the hospital, we were told 'have faith in god' – and I did my best to do that. I wanted to have faith; I truly did – but what I needed was an organ!

As the weeks stretched on, even Pradip bhaiya could not remain in Chennai. Someone besides Maa had to stay with me to handle the many decisions regarding my medications, hospital tests, and the various arrangements that would be required once an organ became available. Maa was helping with food and keeping up the flat; she needed someone else to take care of the medical requirements. It was decided that Shrawan would return and we would reduce our frequent trips to the hospital.

Time continued to pass and our expenses were mounting – the flat was perfect for our needs, but it was costly! We continued to interact with the transplant coordinator, and – mostly out of frustration – we even talked with TNOS executives. We learned that it is not uncommon for people to wait more than a year for a transplant. I have to confess, this news brought my exasperation to a new level. We had initally been told a month, and now it may be more than a year! I began to wonder, 'Why am I here? Six hours is tight, but I could manage to make it from Delhi if an organ became available. Is this worth the extra expense?'

Shrawan too, was frustrated with the delays. Caring for me was not something he was able to do easily, and I could sense that he was eager to get back home. He would have left – I'm sure – but Disha convinced him to stay.

After two months, I got an alert on my phone from the hospital. Immediately I called the transplant coordinator – this was it! We had been waiting for a compatible organ and one had become available. I was told not to eat anything since surgery had to be done within six hours.

My hand was trembling as I handed my phone to Shrawan. I saw that his was too, as he took that and began calling Disha and other family members while we walked to the nearby ATM to get cash. It was night time for Disha in the United States, but she was still awake. Before long all of our family members knew that today was the day I would get a new liver!

We waited anxiously for further instructions from the transplant coordinator. After an hour passed, Shrawan called and was told that although the donor's family had given written consent for the transplant, they were having second thoughts. The transplant coordinator advised that we sit quietly and allow him to try to work with the family.

After Shrawan hung up the phone, my mind was racing from thought to thought. After all this time, could we really get so close just to be denied? The thought seemed unbearable.

Three hours passed… then four. Finally the phone rang… but it was not good news. The coordinator informed us that the family had withdrawn consent. I didn't know whether to be disappointed or relieved not to have the surgery – but we were all mentally exhausted, and we fell into our beds that night for some much-needed rest.

One good thing came out of this close call: we no longer had any doubts that living in Chennai was absolutely necessary. Although a six-hour trip from Delhi to Chennai was possible, we had discovered it would not be possible to travel *and* complete all of the pre-transplant bloodwork necessary. It was good we had not let our frustrations get the best of us.

❖

A key function of the liver is to help maintain the body's immune system by producing Kupffer cells, which cleanse the body of debris such as worn out cells, parasites, and bacteria or fungi.

नीला / *Neela : Blue : bravery and stability; insight, thought*

Every person's life is a roller coaster, with highs and lows. When a serious health condition enters in, however, the ride becomes much more extreme! The person suffering illness or injury is often vulnerable to emotional outbursts in the frustration of having to handle pain or inconvenience – and others surrounding them are affected too.

Pradip bhaivya and Shrawan are Disha's brothers; they are only related to me by marriage. Nothing in my prior experience prepared me for the concern they showed for me and the sacrifices they made. I'm sure they were reluctant at times, but caring for me (and Maa) in our moment of need was the right thing to do, and they were good to do it for Disha and me. I'm proud to be a part of a family of such good men.

When Disha left for the United States, it was difficult for me. I needed my wife beside me. But when we thought an organ transplant was imminent, it was difficult for her to be so far away and helpless. Disha is a lady who knows how to get things done – I am sure she shared our frustrations and mental exhaustion through those events, even from afar.

One thing I know for sure: having Disha's brothers beside me through this ordeal brought us closer as a family, and taught me what it is like to have people in your life who will stick by you and sacrifice in hard times. I needed to learn that lesson in life; and now god has seen to it that I survived to – hopefully – show the same thing to someone else.

Chapter 8

Disha's Return

बैंगनी / *Baingani : Purple : miracles*

I heard the world around me long before I became aware that I had returned. There was a sound of people – some talking, others moaning, some getting sick. In my unconscious state, I almost couldn't grasp that these were real; they seemed to be something distant and unimportant, yet they would not stop and seemed to demand that I return to them.

Someone pushed a curtain near me open or closed, and the noisy rings holding it fast to the rod above it clammered in such a way that it startled me back to semi-consciousness. I started to crack my eyes open, but the light was too bright. Scowling, I raised a hand to shade them, but that failing, I rubbed both fists into my eyes. Immediately, I wished I had not done that – I wished I had stayed unconscious – for the pain I was feeling was not something I wanted at all. But the next thought after that was, 'Hey, I'm alive!'

The joy of that fact – that I had survived the immediate threat of surgery to live another day – caused me to brave the bright lights and open my eyes to look at the world around me. What I saw was a visual equivalent to what I had been hearing – people milling about, nurses and doctors and patients, some talking, others moaning and some getting sick. But even with the unpleasantness, there was an overwhelming joy – a joy just to be allowed to witness life in the world again, no matter its condition.

My mouth was the dryest it had ever been, and I struggled in moving my tongue to make just enough saliva to swallow. When I did, the burning, bruised feeling in my throat was a clear indication that the surgery had, in fact, occurred. Somewhat painfully, I cleared my throat and called to get the attention of a passing nurse. 'May I have some water?' The soreness was enough to prevent me from adding 'please'.

She looked at me kindly and said, 'Of course – just a moment.'

As I felt the cool water slide down my throat, comforting the pain even as it caused it, the wonder of that struck me. In many ways, life is pain – and yet, somehow at the same time, it is a joy to live.

I was still drinking the water when a nurse brought Disha to me. Close behind her were other family members, but in my gratitude, I saw only her: my encouragement, my strength, my life… my wife.

❖

8.1 Disha's return

'You have to come now, Disha.'

I had been sleeping, and in my dazed state, I could hardly believe my ears. It was Shrawan and he was talking to Disha on the phone.

'Ashu needs someone here, and I cannot stay,' he was saying. 'Praivin cannot return. His mother is here, but he needs you.'

I held my breath. Shrawan was speaking the very words of my heart that I did not dare to say, even to myself. Instead, for months I had told myself that Disha must stay in the United States, she must continue to work, she must earn the money our family needed to pay for my stay in Chennai and my eventual surgery. Not once since the early days of her departure had I allowed myself to think of her coming home to me. She was doing what she had to do and I would do what I had to do – even if it meant I had to be without her.

I could not hear Disha's side of the telephone conversation, so there was a long silence. Finally, I released my breath, no longer able to hold it.

'Good,' Shrawan said. 'We will pick you up at the airport.'

I could not believe my ears. Disha was coming to Chennai? How could that be? My mind could not grasp it, but before I could spend any time trying to process it, my entire being was flooded with a gratitude I cannot put into words. This was what I needed most at this moment, when I was feeling terribly sick and helpless. I needed Disha. I needed my beloved wife with me.

Shrawan came into my room just then, carrying a glass of water. I sat up unsteadily, but managed to grab it and gulp it down. As my thirst was quenched, it felt like a physical manifestation of the gratitude I was feeling. I was barely hearing Shrawan's words as he explained to me that he had contacted Disha and told her to come to Chennai.

A few days later, I watched Disha enter the airport, and when our eyes met, there was so much love instantly between us. We had been apart six months, but as I embraced her it felt like we could never be separated. We were filled with a joy that cannot be explained with words, and suddenly I knew my wife could never leave me in my time of need.

'Ashu,' she said, looking into my eyes with love and so much confidence. 'Ashu, before I leave here, you will have your liver.'

I blinked, then searched her face with my eyes. I thought to myself, 'She sounds so confident – how can she know something like that?' I blinked again, then looked down and said, 'Okay.'

'I mean it,' Disha said, moving her head so that she could look me in the eyes again. 'And Ashu, you have to believe it. I want to hear you say it.'

I hesitated. Disha had always encouraged me to have positive thoughts, but this was something new. It was one thing to agree with her; it was another to say something when I was not sure of it.

'Come on,' Disha said. 'Say it and mean it. You can do that.'

I took a deep breath, somewhat uncomfortable. I wanted to sit down somewhere with her, hold her in my arms, share some good food, and make the best of our time together. Finally I decided the only way I could get all of that was to get this over with. I mustered up what little faith I had, looked into her eyes, and said, 'Before you leave Chennai, I will have a liver.'

Disha held my gaze for a moment, and I expected her to make me repeat it again, but instead she nodded and said, 'Yes, good. Now let's go.' She picked up her suitcase, but I reached over and took it from her, thinking, 'I still have enough strength to carry her bag.'

As we made our way through the airport to the car, I reflected on Disha's faith. Always in the past, when she made statements like the one she had just made me repeat, I would pretend to agree, but secretly I did not share her faith. When we were wanting to move into a flat, long before we found one, Disha would say, 'We will find the perfect flat, and it will have lots of space and a good view.' I would think, 'We can't afford such a place.' Yet within a year, everything changed: I got good IT job, Disha got promoted and suddenly we had the income to afford a nice flat. When we found our spacious apartment with balconies and windows on three sides, I couldn't believe it – even as it was happening.

Even now, with the affirmation barely past my lips, I could not help but think of how unlikely it was for me to get a liver within the next few weeks. After all, there were thousands of people on the waiting list, many of whom waited for years to get a liver. I looked over at Disha's face out of the corner of my eye. She looked over, and as soon as her eyes met mine, she smiled a beautiful smile and said, 'Ashu, it's your thoughts that make your destiny.'

I smiled back at her. 'I think I need to travel,' I said. 'For 6 months I have done nothing but watch my diet and go for treatments. Let's go somewhere – that always seems to help me.'

She looked at her watch. 'It's late, Ashu,' she said. 'We'll talk about this tomorrow.'

The next morning, I woke up to find Disha packing my things into a bag. She informed me that Shrawan had planned a short trip for us to Pondi – he had even gained the doctor's approval before Disha arrived. I was surprised that Shrawan had gone to that much trouble, but it did not surprise me that the doctor approved. This was always the response we got in the three years of my treatment. The doctors know how difficult treatment can be, and taking a break with a change of scenery is usually a good thing. If you can relax and get your mind off your troubles, it raises your spirits, which has to have a positive effect on your well being.

We piled into a taxi and headed for Pondi, which is only 90 minutes from Chennai. This was the perfect destination as far as I was concerned: far enough away to feel like a vacation from my treatment, but still close enough that we could make the trip back should I receive an alert about an available organ. The scenery on the way was beautiful, with a magnificent view of the sea on our right.

'We should get a house on this sea,' Disha said.

'If you do, I will visit you,' Shrawan chimed in.

'Yes!' I replied enthusiastically. 'We must do it!' (In my heart, I added, 'If I survive…'; I was well aware this could be my last tour, since even if I did receive an organ for transplant, the surgery was risky.)

When we got to the resort in Pondi, I was amazed at how luxurious it was. The buildings in Pondi are only two to three stories – you won't find any high-rise buildings there. The weather was hot when we arrived, and I was exhausted, so initially we rested for a couple of hours in our room. I wanted to sleep, but we were all hungry, so we decided to check out the hotel's restaurant instead.

'Hey is the lift not working?.' I said to an attendant, finding a way to creep downstairs without making noise.

'Yes sir there is some issue which we are trying to fix. Hopefully it will be done in next few hours.' He replied in a courteous manner.

Lift under repair won't be much of a problem for other guest, I guessed, but for me with acute hyptopulmonary syndrome causing severe breathing issues, it would be tedious to climb up the stairs, although the building was just three-storey and we were required to climb just few stairs to reach the restaurant. It would not involve any potential risk on my health. I thought.

Still Disha made me wait for twenty minutes in a hope that lift would start running. Her being over cautious and caring sometimes made me feel bad.

'Disha let's go to the terrace using stairs. I don't like you to be over caring all the times. It makes me feel I am more of a liability to you,' I said in commanding tone.

Disha nodded sheepishly as we climbed up the stairs.

It was very true. Ever since I was diagnosed with a liver disease Disha had kept me with extra care , her overwhelming cautiousness for my health reminded me of my frailty.I had to depend on her for everything I did. It made me feel incompetent at times. But when I look back, I find her scrupulous care well justified and important to prolong my liver failure in the event of such a fatal disease.

Entering the second floor reception area, we were surprised to find lovely open air terraces with awnings to shield diners from the scorching sun. As I have mentioned, Disha loves to relax on terraces, and due to my health issues, I tried to avoid closed-in crowded spaces, so we settled on a table on the terrace. There was a pleasant breeze, and after a few moments we did not miss the air conditioning at all. We finished our lunch, the whole time enjoying the amazing view of the sea beside us and its soothing sounds. We found ourselves already completely relaxed and we returned to our room ready for some sleep.

'We mustn't sleep too long,' Disha said as she turned down the bed. 'If the sun goes down, we won't be able to see the beach. I want to go for a walk when we wake up.'

'You're right,' I responded, yawning. I believe I was asleep before my head hit the pillow.

After a while, I became aware of Disha and Shrawan busily moving about the room. I slowly sat up on the edge of the bed, rubbing my eyes.

'Is everything okay?' I asked.

'Yes,' she said. 'But the sun is down… we slept too long.'

'It's okay,' Shrawan said. 'We can still enjoy a walk now, and maybe again in the morning.'

'We can,' she agreed. 'I'm also curious about the night life!'

We got ready quickly and headed downstairs, surprised at how few people we encountered in the elevator and the lobby.

'I think you'll get your walk on the beach,' Shrawan said, 'but I'm not sure there's much else in the way of night life!'

He was right. Pondi is deserted at night and hardly any of the shops and businesses stay open. This did not stop us from enjoying the resort, the beach, and the beautiful scenery, which we captured in many photographs.

By this time, my illness had advanced quite a bit – two of my hepatic veins were already completely blocked, severely impacting blood flow from my liver to my heart. At a slow pace, though, I was still able to enjoy myself, and I was grateful for the chance to spend so much time with my wife. Even though we did not adventure much, I consider Pondi to be the most memorable of the trips we have taken.

Our stay was short. Shrawan's flight to Delhi from Chennai was the very next evening. After a restful night we awoke, got ourselves ready, and attended a church service. When it had ended, our hope was to go to the beach again. But the sun was blisteringly hot, so we returned to the hotel for breakfast room service instead. Feeling well fed, well rested and satisfied, we got back into a taxi for the return trip to Chennai. Shrawan needed to get back by noon to pack his things. As we said farewell to the sea, it crossed my mind again that it may be the last time I would see it… the last time I would see Shrawan. Life was becoming a series of potential 'last times'.

I looked over at Disha, who had been watching my face. She reached over and took my hand, and I squeezed hers reassuringly. I did not share my thoughts with her; I knew she would want me to think positively, so I mustered a smile and turned back to the window.

For more than a month after Shrawan's departure, Disha and I made the most of each day, believing that I would go in for my transplant soon – but day after day, the phone did not ring. I had never been one to sleep with my phone, but now I carried it everywhere, always with me, so that I would not miss a single call. Days became weeks, and weeks passed quickly. The day Disha had to return to the United States was fast approaching, and each day, I willed the phone to ring – but to no avail.

With only two days remaining, I began to think of what would be best for Disha before she returned. She is diabetic and is supposed to go for a check-up every three months. While Disha is very fussy over my health, she rarely gives thought to her own condition. I knew she was overdue for her own doctor's visit, so I encouraged her to schedule an appointment at the hospital so she could see someone before her departure.

The day of her appointment, we arrived at the hospital very early in the morning. Disha's blood tests require her to fast overnight, so it's easiest to have them done in the early hours. I sat in the waiting room while they called her back, and was surprised when my phone rang. The Caller ID read 'Coordinator Chennai' – and it took a moment for the meaning of that to sink in. Could this be the call we had been waiting for?

I pressed the button on the phone to answer the call, but I was unable to hear anyone on the other end. My heart was racing, and I felt a bit lightheaded when I stood. Staggering slightly, I tried as quickly as I could to make my way to Disha.

'I'm sorry sir, you can't go in there,' a nurse said, holding out an arm to block my way. I could see Disha in the other room; another nurse was drawing her blood.

'Disha!' I called out, 'Disha, I got a call. I think it's the transplant coordinator!' This was only the second time I had ever received such a call; usually I was the one who had to contact him. 'I'm sure it's him, but the call was dropped!'

'The network in the hospital is always spotty,' Disha called back to me. 'Try WhatsApp instead.' I nodded, already opening the app as the nurse ushered me back to the waiting room.

'Hello?' I heard the coordinator say on the other end of the WhatsApp call.

'This is Ashu,' I said. 'I got a call from you a minute ago.'

'Ashu, yes,' the coordinator said distractedly. 'Yes, please go to the hospital. You need to be there within 30 minutes.' He dropped the call before I could even respond. My mind was still racing – was there an organ, or not?

I sent him a text to let him know I was already at the hospital and he replied saying he would be there shortly. It was so early in the morning, I could not help but start to get excited. He would not call this early if there wasn't an organ.

Disha, as always, was calm. In fact, she continued with her tests without interruption. Minutes passed and soon it had been a whole hour since I had heard from the coordinator. I was getting anxious to text him again when he arrived. As he entered the waiting room, I stood, but before I could speak, he held up both hands as though to stop me.

'There is an organ, Ashu,' he said. 'We want to try to get your surgery done today. I know this is sudden, but you need to be brave and start getting your bloodwork done.'

I stopped in my tracks, hardly believing what I was hearing. I had waited so long for this day; now it was really happening!

Suddenly my mind filled with worry: worry over the transplant, worry over the surgery, worry over the possibility of incompatibility, of infection, of rejection. But after just a moment I caught myself. I turned toward the sample collection room to get my blood tests, and as I walked, I did not show even a hint of worry. Inside my mind I had begun telling myself, 'This is the day everyone has been praying for: your wife, your family, your friends. This is the day Disha told you would come. You must be courageous. You must be fearless and firm. You must believe in a positive outcome.'

It crosses my mind now that Disha and I were both having our blood drawn at the same time, just in separate rooms. Once we were both done, we moved to a lounge to wait for the doctors to arrive.

Dr Joy Vargeese is the director of hepatology in Chennai's global hospital where my surgery was scheduled to take place. It is the best hospital in India for liver transplants – they have a lot of experience and a remarkable record for success with these surgeries. They even hold a Guinness record for having performed a transplant on a five-day-old baby.

I had met Dr Joy several times, and always considered that he is well named. His attitude and behaviour is always positive, polite and cheerful. I will always be most grateful to him for his kindness, compassion, and above all, his skills in treating my illness and removing this bump from the road of my life.

When Dr Joy arrived at the hospital, I was taken to a room near the operation theatre and prepped for surgery. Eventually Disha was permitted to join me, and she did all she could to keep my mind away from the surgery and instead on our future. She talked about all the good food we could enjoy without the food restrictions, about all of the places we would go, all the wonderful things we would see together.

Maa came in briefly, and she was very emotional. Who could blame her? She had already lost her husband and her eldest son and now her only remaining son was undergoing risky surgery. Even so, Disha only allowed Maa a few moments with me, trying her best to maintain the positive atmosphere around me regardless of everyone's concern.

The last thing I remember is the anaesthesiologists, who came in past Disha and checked me for fever before administering anesthesia through a line already inserted into my arm.

'Do you hear that?' one of them said. I was starting to become relaxed but I did hear a siren in the distance. 'That's the ambulance bringing your liver,' he concluded – the final words I would hear before losing consciousness.

❖

8.2 The surgery

My transplant surgery began at 3:30 p.m. on August 1, 2019. It lasted more than 12 hours, concluding at 4:00 a.m. the next morning. A team of at least 20 doctors and innumerable nurses and staff members were involved in this marathon surgery. These were the most crucial 12 hours of my life during which my family remained on edge, calling frequently trying to learn my status.

I remained comatose and senseless throughout my surgery. I wish if I could watch the surgeon perform on my body to remove the bump of my life and cut me and wound me with knifes to make me whole and healthy, but the only last conversation I remember was the doctor telling 'jigar aa gya'. With all my senses benumbed, I could only contemplate with my mind's eye and envisage a successful surgery.

'Hey the patient seems to be anesthetized, please start the process', said Dr rajnikanth, surgeon at Global Hospital.

A squad of doctors encircled around my gurney, they mustered to discuss the proceedings of the operation. They already performed many virtual surgery on me and are aware of my condition.

'The patient seems infection free, no sign of fever. We are good at that part,' said Dr Mahesh – Anesthetic doctor at Global. Everyone in the group agreed.

'The only thing to worry about the patient is acute HPS (hyper pulmonary syndrome), we need to be very careful while operating him, as breathing difficulty can cause heart choke while operating,' Dr Joy added.

Doctors chose the most common technique of liver transplant for me – orthotopic liver transplant – in which the native liver is removed and replaced by the donor organ in the same anatomic position as the original liver.

The surgery can be divided into different stages which includes all the process from incision to closure of incision. I might not follow the technical difficulties of the doctors performing on me but I could follow the fright and pressure on them to perform well that thrived across all the member of team and was reverberating loud in their talks. Out of all the various upper abdominal incisions possible, doctors chose Makuuchi incision (J shaped incision going across lower chest till right most part of abdomen)for me.

Lying on my gurney with my abdomen open, I could only image them with my mind's eye.

'I couldn't have thought of a worst outcome, his liver is in pieces. How is this man still alive?' Dr Rajnikanth howled.

'It is going to be one of the most complicated surgeries we ever did, but we are still optimistic for a successful transplant, as the liver graft lying on the black table is in very good condition,' Dr Joy said motivating the squad.

Successful OLTx is completely dependent on a well-preserved and properly functioning liver. Effective techniques for multiple organ procurement have been developed by TNOS and these have been essential for successful surgery.

'But how to remove the native diseased liver? We are aware there is no single best method to do so, at least we expected a better situation of the organ,' Dr Dargan whined.

'Stop whining! You are making my nerves get the best of me,' Dr Joy said frowning.

'We must muster some courage. We have done more critical cases… it's still an easy one comparatively,' he added.

Removing a diseased organ is by far the most difficult process of the liver transplant, it may be impossible to dissect the structures of the hepatic hilum individually because of massive formation of varices. Controlling of the hepatic arterial and portal venous blood supply are necessary prior to mobilization of the liver from the hepatic fossa to prevent massive haemorrhage.

The most critical time of my surgery is ahead. Will my soul remain in my body or will it liberate itself beyond this world, into the space in the red skies?

The squad remained on their toes for the most turbulent stage ahead when native liver was removed and the inferior vena cave and portal vein were occluded. This can lead to cardiovascular disorders and renal dysfunction.

In the midst of Veno venous bypass (a technique adopted in liver transplant) my heart started sinking. Before long the doctors the doctors syringed me an injection to keep my heart beating. I lost myself in a deep red light which ravished me. A force pulled me away from my body.

Disha felt a very intense jerk prompting a trickling sensation in her heart. Oh god, is everything going well inside? She stood restless. She tried to get the status from inside but no-one was allowed in the operation theatre

She could only pray and send positive thoughts for me, retaining a chair of waiting hall for hours without food and water was something that would even make god to relent his decision of claiming my life. Her unwavering faith provided for me. Before long, I could hear the beep of the machine in the ICU.

'My god, the patient is back,' Dr Joy said pointing towards the ventilator, which showed some scribbled lines.

'Great, he is showing some movement, perhaps we need more dose of general anaesthesia,' Dr Mahesh added.

Few hours later, doctor put the new graft in the same position as was my native liver they already had taken various steps to prevent blood loss. This again was a very complicated process and required lots of skills and only a handful surgeons across the country were capable of performing such intractable surgery.

I couldn't have hoped for a better outcome,' Dr Joy said.

'Ashu may need some additional therapy so that we can prevent the disease getting repeated, but we'll decide that later.

Now that we have completed the surgery, we must save him from any infection,' he added.

'I wouldn't say the operation was a walk in the park, but I'm glad we did it, and I believe it has been cured at this point,' Dr Rajni submitted.

I strongly feel my chances of recovery were the best here at the Global Hospital, Chennai. I don't think there's any other facility that would have done a better job than Dr Joy and his skilled team members.

The doctors kept my status among themselves until the conclusion of the surgery, and even after that the only announcement they sent was:

"The operation was successful and the patient is stable."

I can only imagine the calm and comfort these words brought to my wife, my mother and my family. These words brought to fruition what my wife had steadily held as true from the beginning in unwavering faith.

When I reflect on the six months between my initial diagnosis and the conclusion of my surgery, I can only marvel. Never would I have believed a successful transplant could be possible in that short period of time. Never would I have guessed that we could gather the necessary funds in such short a time. Never would I have thought that my own attitudes about my wife, my life, my family, my doctors and my friends could be so radically transformed.

Each step of the way, it seems as though we moved under god's guidance, doing and saying exactly what needed to be done as it was needed. Fortune favoured us in making an organ available. The entire experience has been magical.

Chapter 9

Recovery

केसरी / Kesari : Saffron : purification; creation, reproduction

It is the day of my liver transplant. Lying on the gurney that will take me to the operating theatre, a shiver runs through my body clothed only in a thin hospital gown. My skin becomes like gooseflesh, and my senses are heightened.

People approach – they are doctors and nurses, but with my eyes closed, this reality fades in my thoughts. My life is on the line today. Before long, people will take knives and cut into my body. They will be doing it to save me – injuring my body, in the hope of making it whole.

For months, I have watched my body deteriorate, weight dropping from my frame day upon day. As the weight has dropped, I have become frail and weakened – I have done my best to carry on, but watching myself slowly transform from a vibrant young man to a frail person near death… well, it has changed me.

Cold cloths begin to wipe my body down, and I am suddenly reminded of the animals being prepared for sacrifice. Cleaning of animals is done with an understanding that god is worthy of a perfect sacrifice – and although we may not be able to perfect the animals, we can at least offer them cleaned. As I feel the cold, wet strokes on my skin, my mind turns to god… to life… and in my spirit, I pray… Today I want to live…

In this heightened state, I hear everything: the traffic on the street, the conversations outside the room, the rustling of the nurse's sleeve as she moves her arm, even the sound of the wipe as it moves along my skin. I smell the antiseptic fluid of the wipes, as well as the lotion they spread over the area where the incision will be. Gently they shave the skin, removing any trace of hair in the hope of keeping the incision as clean as possible.

They are speaking to me, telling me what they are doing and what I can expect, but even without anesthetic, I am already semi-conscious. There is nervousness, of course, but it is a controlled nervousness. My thoughts are my destiny. I must believe for a successful surgery. I want to live…

My eyes open now, I watch the needle for the intravenous line slide beneath my skin. Although there was surely a pin prick along with it, I am unaware of any pain. How funny we are, we people. As a child, I may have cried over the injury of a needle piercing my skin. As a dying young man, I am grateful for it – knowing that it may lead to my healing.

Hearing the door, I turn my head, and there she is. My Disha. My darling wife. Woven through my tangled emotions of fear, courage, weakness, and resolve, I find… an amazing sweetness that fills my being at the very sight of her. I had believed we already said our goodbyes, but here she is again… and I am so… grateful.

We spend our final hours before my surgery in gentle conversation. Our shared dreams of life sustain us in these last moments – we will have a tomorrow. We will enjoy our home... we will continue to travel... we will share glorious meals and wonderful holidays. And in our togetherness... I believe... I will live...

❖

9.1 Recovery

It was just three days since I had undergone a surgery. Lying on my gurney, I was scrolling down my tab. I was overwhelmed with gratitude for everyone who has helped me cross this bump in my life. I could not stop thanking Dr Joy and his team at Global hospital for making this intractable surgery a success. The nursing staff at Global for taking wonderful care of me throughout my hospitalization, I could remember I was very hard to handle at times, the side effect of some steroids given to me made me uncooperative and aggressive but the attendants at Global hospital were very professional ,they never bothered about my behaviour and cared for me with compassion. My eyes were filled with tears lest I hid my emotions under my smile. Disha and her family did a lot for me and I was trying to write something for expressing my gratitude to them. I wanted to express my feelings to everyone my wife, my family, my doctor and even my company FSG. With these thoughts wheeling in my mind, I did not notice a team of doctors coming into my room to observe me. I was still in ICU, my body had several wounds following immediate surgery, there were two lines or tubes placed in my belly for draining out the waste – they called them drain line and calculated the drain every four hours. They also put a central line through my neck – (A tube placed in the large vein in the neck to give fluids, blood or medication or to do medical test quickly) adding the discomfort further an oxygen mask was placed on my nose to keep a check on my saturation point which remained low continuously.

With all these lines I looked more like an electric circuit with intricate tubes all across my body, the pain was immense, yet the joy of survival was enough to override it. I raised my hand towards the doctors to catch their attention and gestured to express my gratitude by nodding my head and making a V sign ought to show my happiness by indicating the victory over the deadly disease. Seeing me the doctor could understand I was having discomfort with the oxygen mask and instructed nurse to replace it with the nasal pipe. Retaining the same posture since last five days strained my back and I was glad when finally the doctors advised mobilization for me. The attendants arranged the sofa in a jiffy and placed it right beside my gurney. I settled on the sofa with the help of nurse and other attendants. I was now ready to meet my wife. Seeing me sitting and browsing on my tab would only make her feel ecstatic.

Visiting hours in the ICU were fixed, I had to wait for hours before I could meet with my family that too for a very short time. I had to say a lot to my wife, but every time I saw her I could not speak more than what she actually asked, the visiting time was too short for a casual conversation, but today I had to say how much I loved her and how grateful I was for her support. I even asked for permission for a slightly longer stay from the supervisor and she approved that. I was seated on the sofa for about an hour before it was time for Disha to come. I could see her coming through the hallway, she was wearing a mask and a hospital gown, as nobody was allowed to enter the ICU without wearing those essentials. The hospital staff was very strict about their hygiene practices and practiced conducive methods to make the place infection-free. Disha entered the room. I asked her to pull a chair from the nursing station, my voice was low yet she understood. I could feel the happiness in her eyes, she was joyful to see me sitting. It was enough evidence that I was recovering well for everyone in my family. Before I could start my conversation with Disha, doctors arrived again. This time Dr Joy was heading them, he first turned over my reports kept on the nursing station of the ICU then scooted closer to Disha to discuss my recovery. I could overhear their discussion. Having googled about the disease I could understand all the parameters of the report, except TAC levels. It was something I had never heard of before, but the doctor instructed the nurse to take the sample of TAC every 12 hours. Later he moved towards me to ask about my health, he observed me with his stethoscope checked my vitals and explained that all my parameters were settling well.

'Hey Ashu, how are you doing, you look more strengthened now. Your reports are showing well and I am very happy for you.' Dr Joy said.

'What is in the report sir, I heard you saying my bilirubin level was still high, I maintained a low level of platelets count and my albumin and INR level is still soaring how could you say I am doing well,' I asked in an inquisitive way.

I knew I could ask anything to him, he was very humble and generous in his behaviour.

'Well Ashu what I meant was that your parameters are improving. It would be unreal if I say you can get back to normal just in a few days after the surgery. The body takes its own time for recovery, it's not like putting a battery in a dead phone and expecting it to play as you wish too. Don't worry you will be good in some time.'

By the time he finished the visiting time was over. Disha had to go back and my wish to express my feelings extended to yet another day. But now I knew I will live another day and every other day coming in our future. I could express my love tomorrow. The freight and shivering of my survival were gone long before. Disha couldn't come close to me but waved her hands to bid goodbye. The nurse made me stretch on my gurney as I fell asleep in minutes.

The next day as I got up I could see some doctors discussing to remove my central line the tube across my neck was causing lot of discomfort to me and I wanted to get rid of it sooner. They saw me awake and one of them asked.

'Hey Ashu, we will be removing the tube from your neck today. We want you to start walking, you are doing good and if your conditions remain stable for another four days, we would discharge you from the ICU.'

I knew it was important to walk after the surgery. I have read ambulation promotes blood flow of oxygen throughout the body while maintaining normal breathing functions, improved blood flow stops the development of any blood clots and aids in quicker wound healing. I immediately provided my consent to walk and replied.

'Yes, I would love to walk.'

The doctor smiled and asked me to wait for some time and instructed the nurses to remove the central line.

Oh, how much more pain do I need to suffer from, I thought, but the discomfort of the tube across my neck was even more painful and I wanted to get rid of it at a time. I called the nurse immediately to remove it.

'Please wait for some time sir and have your lunch before removal of the tube. You may feel an unpleasant sensation for some time and won't be able to have your lunch.'

'Please remove this now, I can have my food after some time.' I screamed.

I wanted to liberate myself from all the tubes across my body. With central line removed I could at the minimum nod my head freely, while talking to someone.

The sister called two of her assistants to help her remove the tube. They held me so that I couldn't move.

'Relax Ashu and take long breaths,' she said while pulling out the tube from my neck.

A stinging pain ran across my body when the tube was removed, the burning sensation remained for some time making the words of sister true. I couldn't eat my lunch.

'Let's go for a walk sir,' asked one of the physiotherapists rousing me from a deep sleep.

'Sure, let's go,' I replied.

I stepped out of my gurney and staggered on my feet to sway a little step. The attendants held me and caught the drain bags attached to the tube placed in both the side of my stomach. I started walking. This little walk of two minutes made me feel as if I have triumphed in my fight for life, the joy of walking for minutes was more than standing first in a race during my school. The doctors clicked some of my photographs while walking, they took it to advertise their achievement in the press and sent some of those to Disha.

It became more of a routine since then, when the physiotherapist would knock me for a walk randomly several times during a day and it continued throughout my hospitalization. Ten days of intensive care were enough for me when the doctors decided to transfer me to a private ward. The room stay would make me more reachable to my family, but at the same time, it could also make me more vulnerable to infection. The hospital administration left no stone unturned to prevent any cause of infection and even now anyone entering my room had to wear a mask.

Within the ambit of privacy of our personal room, it would be easy to express my feelings to Disha. I had gained some strength in the last few days of my hospitalization and had become a voracious eater with my muscles starting to build up. Eating too much is very common after liver transplant, so I didn't have to worry over my eating habits. With the increased strength, I was now able to raise my voice to Disha a few steps away from my gurney.

'Hey Disha, we made it at last,' I said. I wanted to embrace her warmly to show my love for her. I could see her happy, she gave a smile but routed our conversation to a different topic.

'How humble she is!' I mused.

'Do you like the food given here?'

'Yes dear,' I replied.

The restrictions of oil and salt were over and I liked anything that was prepared with salt in it. I learnt the significance of adding salt in food as every meal I got was bland and salt free during my illness. Food given to me in the hospital was richer in protein. I enjoyed the delectable food a lot and awaited every serving. Disha would usually order for me, asking me what I would like to have.

During my hospitalization, writing became my hobby. Whenever I didn't find anyone around me to talk to, I started putting my emotions to words. I also went through some of the books of renowned authors which instilled in me various ideas of creative writing.

When I shared my notes of gratitude with Disha, she strongly felt I should write more and give it the form of a book.

The doctors were happy seeing me engaged, they wanted the patients to be vibrant during recovery. These twenty-one days of my hospitalization were unlike other times of my life. But even then, I enjoyed it thoroughly and I treasure it. I triumphed my victory over my disease and even enjoyed dancing and waving my hands in happiness while still in the hospital. I wish I could share the videos of my dance.

Sitting on the sofa, I was humming my favourite song, since I was to be discharged today.

'Ek pyaar ka nagma hai.' And true it was.

Life indeed is a flow of love, the flow of ecstasy and you have to steal a full life from moments.

I had to stay in Chennai for some more time, my tubes were removed before discharge, but the drain bag was still placed and pasted over the wound where the tube was actually inserted on my belly, which collected the drains. The wounds of my surgery were still pinned and required frequent dressing. We had to visit the doctors twice a week. The doctors mainly tested TAC levels, tests usually done on transplant patients to measure the amount of drug in the blood to determine whether it has reached a therapeutic level and is below the toxic level. Immunity suppression drugs were given to me so that my body didn't reject the new organ. High level of steroids were also given to me. All in all, the number of medicines I took could be compared to a small meal, but I was happy even with that.

Disha didn't let anyone enter our house, not even the maid or cook were allowed. She did all the household work herself along with her professional commitments. She continued to work from home so as to suffice our income.

Whenever I expressed my interest to start my work, she would not let me switch on my laptop. I could start my work only after the doctor's approval, which I got after forty-five days of my surgery.

Living with my wife during my recovery is something I would always rejoice in my life. The memories may fade away, but our love would remain immortal.

❖

9.2 Getting back to normal

Forty odd days of my surgery had passed. I was happy enjoying my recovery with the most adorable person I would ever have. I was loving Disha's company. Despite the work from home privilege, I soon wanted to get back to my work. I had been away from my wife for a very long time due to my illness, but now as I was getting better, I had to find ways to start living together. It was not wise for Disha to abandon her job and a she had earned wonderful opportunity. I needed to find some ways out for relocation. Doctors already approved that I could go anywhere I wanted. With all these thoughts swirling in my mind, I heard a charming voice of my wife.

'Ashu … Ashu ….' She called from the kitchen.

'Yes dear,' I replied.

'Did you book the cab for the hospital? We have a routine check-up scheduled today,' she inquired.

'Ohh Dishu, I am sorry, I forgot.'

'You are invariably irresponsible Ashu. I was expecting something similar from you. So I booked it in advance yesterday.

Did you have your medicine?' she screamed.

'Yes, I took those.'

'I wonder, how I would survive without you dear? You are amazing. Let's go, I need to ask a lot from the doctor today.' I tried to distract her to cover my miss.

Upon reaching the hospital, I turned over the pages of my report which I had collected from the counter.

'Hey Disha, the bilirubin level is normal, except for INR all the parameters seem to be good, I am expecting doctors will grant approval to our plead of relocation to Noida today,' I said joyfully.

'I wish it so happens; it has been two months I am in India. I need to get back to work.' She said.

Even though I was aware that Disha needed to go back, the words fell harsh on my ears. Now that I was healthy, I wondered why she needed to go back.

The doctors approved my relocation and we went back to Delhi.

I knew Disha's professional commitment would part us again. But this time I was happy to bid her goodbyes as I knew sometime later, I would join her and we will again rejoice in life.

Ever since my surgery, I had some time to consider my future as I rebuilt my strength. I had written this manuscript and in reviewing my life, I see some interesting patterns.

There is the obvious pattern of liver disease itself. My father developed the disease in large part due to reliance on alcohol to cope with life's difficulties. I also relied on drinking for an escape –

though not for a long time – but I developed the disease for entirely different reasons. Liver disease claimed Papa's life; someone else lost their life to make it possible for mine to be saved.

Then there is the pattern of the men in my family, progressively succumbing to illness and death. First Baba, who died even in the process of having his health checked. Then Papa, whose death still haunts me – perhaps even more so now, knowing what should have been done to provide him better care. Also my brother, who died so suddenly and unexpectedly. We could hardly accept it. And finally my illness, and the miraculous process by which I have been healed.

I have read of survivor's guilt – people who wonder how or why they have been spared when others have lost their lives and I suppose some readers may be asking if this is something I have suffered as well. I have an answer for them: I was not spared to carry guilt over it. I cannot explain why I still have my life when others in my family do not. I can only say that it is for a reason and a purpose. I like to think that it is to help ensure that the pattern of love and generosity lived by my father – and in my wife and her family – will be carried forward to future generations.

Another pattern I have seen is within myself – my past approaches to difficulties in my life, and life's progression of bringing me around to a better way. When my Baba died, I was devastated, and my Papa had to take it upon himself to keep me moving forward. When Papa died, the devastation came again, and it was my brother, Maa and Fua who came together to ensure that I could continue in life.

My brother's death was shocking and difficult – particularly because he was so young. But in observing his wife's family as they surrounded her, it exposed me to something I had not realized before: the importance of family in times of loss – not just for financial support, as I had received, but also love and emotional encouragement.

By the time my own illness took hold of my life, I was well aware of a lack of these things among my own family members. I had seen them disperse after Papa's death; I had heard their whispers during my struggles in college; I had known their rumours and speculations about the cause of my illness. This was not love and support. To me, it was judgment and abandonment.

When I married Disha, I gained so much more than I could have guessed. Not only did I gain a wife with strength, faith, wisdom, and courage (as Fua had predicted), I also gained an extended family that understood the importance of supporting one another, not only financially, but emotionally and spiritually, too. Maa and I have been blessed to become an important part of this group of loving and supportive people – a family whose members extend to one another the benefit of doubt and are willing to make personal sacrifices on behalf of one another. I will never forget Pradip bhaiya, Shrawan and their families in all the assistance they gave Disha and me through my illness. They showed me what family is truly about – something I have no doubt my Papa would have explained to me as I matured.

Through all of this, the key lesson I learnt was that we must accept the reactions of other people, regardless of whether or not we can understand them or relate to them. Each person has a story, just as I have mine. Each person has had good times and bad, joy and pain. When someone reacts unexpectedly – such as not being generous or kind – it is usually because of suffering in their life.

Understanding this makes it easier to allow people to be just who they are, and to forgive reactions that cause us pain. In a way, we can view it as helping them carry their pain, if we can accept the fraction of it that they share with us in the right spirit.

❖

The liver is the only organ in the body to be able to regenerate. It can be cut down to a quarter of its regular size and still regrow to full strength. A living person can donate half their liver, and it will regrow to full size in just over two weeks.

Today, I live. I am healthy and growing stronger every day. I continue my work in Noida and Disha continues hers in the United States. We are a world apart, but in our hearts, we are always together. Video calls allow us to see each other, and texts let us share little things throughout the day. This is not like other couples – but one thing we share the most that young couples do not: we have faced death together, and chosen life.

Epilogue

As I soar above the streets of Delhi, I feel a sense of great gratitude swelling in my heart. Below are my people, celebrating Holi with glorious food and vibrant colours. I fly high above them, my arms outstretched like wings. I look toward my right arm and see it indeed is a wing – with feathers of many colours. I swing my eyes to my left to see a wing there as well. I ponder over this for a moment, then make a decision. 'It does not matter if I'm a bird,' I say, '...or an angel, or just a man with wings – what matters is, I'm alive and I'm flying!' I dart through a few of the plumes of steam rising from the thelas, then fly high, swoop down again, and do a loop in the air. 'I could get used to flying,' I think.

As I sail over the crowd, I hear snippets of their conversation. None of them seem to see me – they laugh in celebration together, and as I move from group to group, their voices seem to be telling a story: a story of life, of love, of happiness and of joy.

Below the crowd I hear a single voice humming. It is a female voice, so quiet I can barely make it out – but it is distinctive and clearly different from the rest of the crowd to me. I tilt my head, trying to hear what song she is humming, and quickly I recognize the voice: it is my Disha, humming a tune we both enjoyed together.

'Tu dhaar hai nadiya ki, mein tera kinara hun... tu mera sahara hai, mein tera sahara hun...' which means you are my support, and I am yours.

I look directly below me, and there she is: my wife, surrounded by our children. They are playing with colour, and having such a good time. I want to join them. I begin to wonder if I know how to land, and I try to move my feet beneath my body to prepare. Before I can descend, I feel sheets against my skin… then a pillow beneath my head… and I know I have been dreaming once again.

Sniffing the air, I recognize the smell of malpua and I know Disha is preparing food for our own Holi celebration. Wistfully, I consider my dream: how many children will we have? Before I can give this any further thought, she calls me.

'Ashu, come try this!'

'Coming!' I call back joyfully, knowing that this year, the food for us will be as full and as rich as any I have ever tasted. No longer will we be restricted from eating foods rich with oil and salt. No longer will I be weakened and confused. My body is once again whole, and life is again glorious – even more so, because I now know how much I have taken for granted.

Quietly I sneak into the kitchen behind Disha, who is turning food in a pan. As I touch her shoulders, I lean close to her ear and whisper, 'You are amazing, Disha.'

'I know that,' she says simply, feigning indifference to my words. 'Now set the table.'

Before I can begin to express mock disappointment at her lack of reaction, she turns and gives me that beautiful smile of hers, and it is like water to my soul. Looking deeply into her eyes, I see her love for me, and all my feelings of disappointment are replaced with my love for her. I gently squeeze her shoulders, steal a small kiss from her lips and turn to do as she requested.

Disha turned, holding a bite of food on a fork in her hand. 'It is delicious, if I do say so myself.' She smiled that beautiful smile I have come to treasure, and popped the bite into my mouth. The scrumptious flavor spread across my tongue before I even had a chance to chew hot and crispy malpua. I mumbled, mouth full. 'It's… tasty.' I chewed the bite, reveling in the celebratory flavors, which seemed familiar.

'It was my favourite dish of Holi – malpua, deep fried in oil and dipped in suger syrup, I could not stop at a single bite to devour it.

As I swallowed the bite, my stomach grumbled, and I realized that I was truly hungry for malpua for first time in years. 'Is there more?' I asked. Not waiting for her answer, I took more from the tray kept beside the frying pan.

Disha laughed. 'You're such a foodie.'

'Don't eat it all, it's not just for you. It's very hard to prepare the dough of this recipe. We are expecting some guests today, and will serve them later. You have some with them.' She said moving away from the kitchen to attend a call.

No sooner I completed my breakfast and sat down on the sofa to relax, I felt a hit of cold water on my left shoulder. Stunned, I froze, then instantly turned my head to face its source. Standing on the door was Aradhya.

'Here she comes,' I yelled in excitement seeing Aradhya, Chandani and Abhinav.

'Come out,' she shouted as she ducked back toward the hallway. She began whistling happily, her tune fading as she made her way back to the to the crowd downstairs.

'They are here, Disha,' I screamed to pull her attention towards us, welcoming Chandani and Abhinav aloud.

The awaited guests arrived, now I would get more malpua to eat, I thought.

Before we could understand, Disha rushed into the hall with a bucket filled with colour and launched a bucket of colour into the air. The stream of water fell, mostly splashing Chandani, but also sending droplets of crimson across the clothing of nearly everyone in the group.

'It's all wet Disha,' I said.

'As if we care. Come on let's play colours,' said Disha.

'More malpua first,' I said playfully tilting my head.

'You are always hungry, Ashu. You first come downstairs to the crowd, and let's have some fun,' Disha said laughing.

Chandani stood frozen on her toes, she didn't expect such a splash from Disha, she couldn't wait to take her revenge and poured the left over colour from the bucket over Disha. We were all wet before long. We went downstairs for colour play where Aradhya and Shrawan were already covered with colour.

Yet again my life is colourful. Like the colours during Holi, the events of our lives paint a vibrant work of art. Every colour symbolizes different phases of life. Disha's faith and commitment, has made the colours of my life more vibrant.

I always considered love to be associated with admiration, we love each other for the physical or psychological virtues, we fall for either beauty, intelligence or other virtues in our partner. This experience in life has taught me another view of love 'generosity'. Love in this context is not a thrill in the face of accomplishments and desires, it's a skill to seek beyond partner's outer dimensions into their experiences in life to bestow forgiveness and kindness and to be generous in spite of trickiness of life. Disha had been very kind to me, she gave me all her attention, time and money. She loved and doted on me at every stage of my life. She affirmed that I will be doing good the day I was diagnosed with deadly disease, I credit her faith and positivity that turned away all odds from our life and even made god to relent and bow to her unwavering faith. I owe her a lot to be able to stand again in life to fulfill our shared dreams and aspirations and yet again we will enjoy glorious meals and wonderful holidays and above all – togetherness.

We have to board a flight tomorrow. I am traveling to the US with Disha and our dreams of togetherness are turning true. Everyone in our family is very happy for us. But every time I look back, I am reminded of the generosity of my wife and I believe it is a key for a prolonged relationship. To sustain healthy and long relationships, we need to explore generosity in love.